Joe's Black T-Shirt

Short Stories About St. Louis

3-15-2011

To Joe,

Life is short.
Stories are forever.

Joe

Joe's Black T-Shirt
Short Stories About St. Louis

By Joe Schwartz

Copyright © Joe Schwartz, 2009

Cover art by Chris Holden, 2009

All rights reserved. No part of this publication may be reproduced, stored in a retrieval system, or transmitted, in any form or by any means, electronic, mechanical, photocopying, recording, or otherwise, without prior permission by the author.

A Stabco Publication
ISBN 978-0-578-03585-7
August 2009

All of the stories included in this manuscript are the work of fiction. Names, characters, places, and incidents either are the product of the author's imagination or are used fictitiously, and any resemblance to actual persons, living or dead, business establishments, events or locales is entirely coincidental.

Dedication

This book is dedicated to the three women in my life in whose absence this book would fail to exist.

First and foremost, my mother, who taught me that the power in the creative art of storytelling is the suspension of disbelief.

Second, in order only, is my lovely wife, Rhonda. I will be forever indebted to her as she showed me that I was not the horrible son-of-a-bitch I thought.

Third, is my editor and friend, Julie Failla Earhart, my cheerleader and staunchest critic.

To each of you, I say thank-you. I love you, and God bless you for putting up with me.

    Joe

Contents

Slow Motion	3
Good Intentions	12
Humidity	25
Ademption	32
Take It Or Leave It	48
3 Pigs and A Dog	62
Father's Day	86
Walking Uphill	96
No More Bets	103
Free Advice	114
Blackwater Opera	120
Family Business	139
Road to Hell	148

Dear Reader:

    If you are reading this I will presume you to have a disaffected spirit by the very definition that is the stylish, yet dissident black t-shirt. Be it for a band or a high-octane motorsport, it is not clothing as much as a statement of values. Whether it is brand new or thread bare, it represents your deepest, inner reflections. It should act as a warning to the happy, go-lucky set that you can be dangerous if provoked.

    These stories are written especially for you. Each one is an effort to tap into that secret psyche that does not conform to society's rules. Rules that don't apply to an underclass struggling to survive in that gray area between indigence and working class poor, standards that have become corrupt and inconceivable as our technology begins to exceed our humanity. These stories are not about people with choices as much as they are about people learning to live with the consequences of actions. That's not to say we move unconsciously, not understanding the eventual outcomes of our self-destructive behavior, it is more about the fact that we simply do not care.

    My own life is a collection of black t-shirts. Occasionally, I must weed items that no longer suit my state of mind. Others though, I have had since I was a teen-ager and could shit-can only if it were about to disintegrate. They are the story of my life. The sense of empowerment I receive from one is equal to the disdain of another. They are all precious in my sight. The most significant are those given to me by close friends. I have never received any higher endowment of respect. Likewise, I offer this collection of short stories to you.

    All these stories are set in St. Louis, a place that I have loved, hated, reviled, and embraced. In short, it is my home. I have been to many other cities that were flourishing megalopolises. The clean streets, friendly locals, their astonishing monuments and museums, and endless variety of amusements only made me homesick.

    St. Louis is a natural landfill of acutely angry people. The town is still a war zone divided by race and money that has hardly changed since I was a boy. Oddly enough, I have grown comfortable within these dire conditions.

    I hope that you will see a neighbor, a co-worker, or even yourself in these words. Most important, I hope you will realize that you are not alone. There are other 'normal people' with the same inconsolable thoughts of desperation and malice hidden behind the thin veil that is a black t-shirt.

    Once you've read it, give it to somebody else as a gift validating the adage that it is the thought that counts.

Acrimoniously yours,
    Joe

Slow Motion

I first decided to kill Edgar last summer.

He had come into all our lives three years ago. There wasn't anything that odd or outstanding about him I could recall. He was a hard worker who didn't need much instruction to get a job done. When the supervisor asked what we all thought of bringing him aboard full time, none of us had any reason to balk.

The kind of work I do is grunt labor. Digging holes, mowing grass, painting buildings inside and out. It's good honest work that doesn't require brains. It's harder than hell to get on full time in a unit, and I spent two years in part-time limbo hoping to get my spot. Over the last ten years, I've learned the mechanics of small engine repair and mower-blade sharpening and mastered the skill of pulling trailers of any size. Even in my chosen profession they are all things unexpected of a woman. Most of the women hired know they don't have to take this serious. We work for the city. The local government is as bound as the largest federal entity to ensure a fair and equal workplace. Every shop has a woman, a black, and, occasionally, a cripple. Generally speaking, we're equally despised.

I refused to be quarantined in the shop while my coworkers, the men, went out to do the real work. Besides, they had to do something with me. After two weeks of leaving me behind, I had reorganized the shop twice and power scrubbed the maintenance yard, removing years of tractor grease and truck oil. That night over a thirty-pack of beer, they decided to give me a real job.

Next morning I sat between the shop steward and the plumber. With every turn the obese plumber's girth shifted onto me. His smell covered me like a fine mist that I could not ignore or get used to.

It was a short ride, maybe five or six miles, to the job site. A bathroom had become 'inoperable' over the winter break.

I had two jobs. To go back and forth to the truck for everything and to shovel shit. The plumber took great delight in berating my inexperience. "Jesus wept," he would say as if divine intervention could help me. "Why don't ya go bake some cookies, Martha, and leave the real work to the men." Then he would laugh and send me back to the truck on another fool's errand. When the back-flow of human waste would inevitably rise, forming an ankle deep black pool of curd-like discharge, I would wade in with my coal shovel, scoop up the watery slop into my wheelbarrow, and dump it out in the woods, downhill behind the cinder-block building. By the end of the day, the problem was diagnosed as a dead possum in the main line. As we rode back to the shop in silence, the plumber's odor no longer bothered me.

The smell of human waste dogged me for three days after. I lost twelve pounds that week, hardly able to swallow a bite of food. Even my menthol cigarettes did little to disguise the awful taste. The guys all made friendly jokes with me about it until eventually I could laugh too, as if it had happened to someone else.

Then little by little they began to show me different things. Simple things like how to mix oil and gas or how to sharpen the chain saw with a rattail file. Complicated things like making concrete from raw materials or felling a tree safely. It gave me confidence to do these things. It made me a better mother to my two sons and it proved to myself that I could do anything if given the opportunity.

It was all so good until Edgar came around. He was somebody's brother-in-law, but we didn't give that much consideration. If you couldn't hack the work as a seasonal laborer, you were gone, regardless if you were first cousin to the Pope himself. After you went full time, it was damn near impossible to get fired. Until we offered him the full-timer's position, he was a model employee.

***

The bing-bong of an electric door chime signaled my entry into the store. Walls of rifles and shotguns stood erect behind the counter with rows of handguns under the glass countertop. The clerk was of indeterminate age, slender with a thick beard. With his coke-bottle thick glasses, his appearance reminded me more of a librarian than an arms dealer.

"Might I help you ma'am," he drawled in a thick southern accent.

"You might," I said. "Are you Ricky Larry?"

"Sure 'nuff," he said. "'Course most folks don't usually seem concerned wit' such."

"I'm John Roberts." I said. The name was a code. It had cost me forty dollars in draft beer and a hand job inside the Tinker's Dam men's room handicapped stall to get it. Now that I was here, I could only hope my spit-shine hadn't been in vain.

"Don't say," he said. "What can I do for ya', John?"

He pushed a button under the counter and an electronic lock bolted the front door. Ricky Larry sat a square cardboard container on the counter with the words SMITH & WESSON printed boldly across. Inside was a used .38 caliber, with rust on the barrel and a thick wad of duct tape wrapped around the handle that looked like it would fall apart the first time the hammer dropped.

"What ya' think?"

"I think," I said, "that I'll pass."

"This here is a right good pistol. Despite the cosmetics."

I stared at him, not buying his song and dance about how this gun was only used on Sundays by a little old lady to shoot gallery targets.

"You might as well unlock the door," I said

"Hold your horses. I got another," he said putting another identical box on the counter. When he lifted the lid, I knew it was exactly what I wanted. A flat black-on-black 9mm Beretta that was no doubt military issue with the markings on the slide and the butt obliterated.

I picked it up and pulled the slide back with ease. The hollow chamber was clean, and the smell of fresh gun oil was overpowering as a barfly's cheap perfume. The weight was well balanced in my hand. I squeezed the trigger and the slide clamped shut with efficiency.

"How much?"

"That there is a good piece, a bona fide sidearm of the U.S. military. A rare item under such circumstances."

"How much?" I asked again. If my experience buying used cars was anything akin to this, I knew the more he talked the more it would cost. The trick was getting him to shut up and pin him down to a firm price.

"Well," he said pondering, trying to accurately gauge my breaking point, "you seem like a nice lady. What ya say, nine hundred?"

"Four hundred," I immediately countered.

"Now look here," he said as his tone lost its friendly, country boy appeal, "this ain't no durn flea market."

"Seven-fifty," I said putting my maximum offer on the table.

He combed his beard with his fingers. Eyes that looked too big for his face through the magnification of the lenses stared into mine, trying to determine if I was bluffing.

Through the cloak of thick facial hair, he smiled wide. His teeth were the shade of a Calico cat. "Gawd-dog! Ya drive a hard bargain, lady, but I do believe that's a fair deal."

I gave him the money, and he put the gun into a dark blue plastic bag. The weapon's weight in my purse made me nervous and happy all at once. I held my purse on my lap all the way back home.

The boys were playing video games when I got home. The teenagers needed little from me in the way of survival. After I fixed hamburgers and skillet fries for supper I told them I had a bad headache and was going to bed early. I locked my bedroom door even though there wasn't a chance I would be disturbed.

My ex loved guns, liquor, and kicking my ass. It was a blessing when the police picked him up driving drunk with a loaded shotgun in the passenger seat. He got five years, and I got a no-fault divorce by a sympathetic judge.

His brother came by and collected his few belongings. He left behind anything he knew he couldn't sell for beer money or trade for truck parts. Had he bothered to open the ladies shoebox at the bottom of the closet he would've been happier than a sissy with a new dick.

I pulled out the pink and white box and set it on the bed next to me. Its lid off, I suddenly felt a bit perverse. Bright red shotgun shells and long silver rifle cartridges lay in a disorganized puzzle but among the chaos was a neat three-by-six rack of gold bullets ready for use. I took one out and examined it. The acronym '9MM' was clearly stamped into the flat, circular base.

I discharged the empty magazine from the gun and re-loaded it full back into the gun's handle. The change was significant. A surge of potency overcame me as I swung the loaded barrel towards the mirror and faced myself. I remembered why in the hell I was doing all this and the thrill evaporated. Edgar.

There was no doubt as to his stealing. The police found our chop saw at First Star Pawn with the ID tag still attached. Posthole diggers, the tamper, and a gas-powered hedge trimmer all suddenly disappeared in conjunction with Edgar getting keys to the shop.

One morning after all the trucks mysteriously wouldn't start, it became clear all the gas had been siphoned. Edgar called in sick that morning and the following day. He had swallowed more than he had stole and had the balls to claim he had the flu although it was the middle of August. It wasn't any skin off our noses though. We figured that given enough rope, it was only a matter of time before he hung himself.

With Edgar though, it was always something. Maybe half your lunch came up missing or your new work gloves that you bought last weekend were nowhere to be found. It made us mad as hell, but we let it go. Sometimes we would get even by deliberately putting him on the trash run in the rain or lending him out to other units in the area for general labor. More often than not, though, he couldn't or wouldn't apply but the most minimal effort. After six months, his reputation preceded him and no other unit except ours would tolerate him. Most days we left him on shop duty where he either watched TV or slept. As long as he didn't bother us, didn't interfere, we were willing to accept it.

That is until Big Mike, the finest heavy equipment operator I had ever known, accused him of stealing a bottle of cologne from his locker. We could all smell the expensive scent on Edgar, but he firmly wouldn't give in. When Big Mike took hold of him by the collar and drug him like a dog outside, we silently followed. There on Edgar's truck seat, you could plainly see the clear bottle we all recognized as

Big Mike's, yet he would not confess. First he said he found it. Then he said it was always there. Finally he told Big Mike he could kiss his ass. The accumulation of lie upon lies compounded into a boiling frustration with which we were all too familiar. Big Mike did what we all had wanted to do many times and punched the little weasel square in the nose. Blood gushed out and stained his shirt. Without a word, Edgar got in his truck and peeled rubber out of the lot.

Half an hour later, celebrating over beers, Edgar's battered pick-up returned accompanied by a police cruiser. Big Mike was arrested, charged with assault and hauled off. A week later the charges were dropped on the stipulation Big Mike immediately resign his position. That's when we quit talking to Edgar. You would think such a collective cold shoulder would shame a man into quitting but not him. He seemed even happier.

The winter passed without many incidents. Occasionally he would come in reeking of the disputed cologne trying to taunt us somehow into another altercation. None of us dared. We all had families and there wasn't a one of us who could replace this kind of money. We were trapped, waiting on the elusive golden rule of eighty. That was when your age plus the time on the job equaled eighty years. If you could make it, sixty percent of your paycheck was yours for the next twenty years, no questions asked. We were in effect marking time and trying to make it as pleasant as possible.

When spring came, we were all eager to escape the drudgery of the shop. With the April showers and the May flowers came the community service workers. Generally, college kids caught driving drunk or smoking pot or both. I was always glad to see them. Most were polite, called me ma'am until I told them otherwise, and were damn good workers. In my entire career, I never saw one two seasons in a row.

It was a rainy morning when Cindy showed up on our door, soaked to the bone, wearing a black tank top tucked into Daisy Duke shorts, and paper-thin thongs. She couldn't have been less ready for a hard day's work if she were nude. Our supervisor was a born-again believer who didn't have a judgmental bone in his body. He decided that she could work until lunch with Edgar at the shop. Certainly she could sweep and mop. Edgar, in a rare display of conscientiousness, assured him 'the young lady would not be shown any special privileges.' The matter settled we walked single file out the door.

When we pulled back into the yard for lunch, the rain had turned into a mist that was cool to the skin but left you dry. Rainbows shimmered in the oil slicks and made the charcoal asphalt beautiful. Cindy looked like she had been crying. I sat down next to her with my paper sack lunch, asked her if she wanted half of my pb & j but she shook her head no. Edgar sat on a bucket in the corner with that smile of his on full blast, staring at her.

The next day, she came in wearing enough layers for snow removal. Call it woman's intuition or simply the experience of living with bad men for far too long, but it was clear to me. Cindy's eyes that had danced with the light of life were now nothing more than extinguished remains. When Edgar deliberately bumped into her, I thought she might scream.

Before the supervisor could speak, I insisted that I was in terrible need of a helper, probably for all week, and that Cindy suited my purposes. Edgar almost objected, then saw how serious I was.

I let Cindy sit in my truck all week, bringing extra cigarettes for her and in general letting her be. Sometimes I would look over and she would be crying or praying or screaming with the windows rolled up. Sometimes I think it was all three at once.

At the end of the week, her hours completed, she surprised me. Arms wide open, she covered me whole and hugged me with more compassion than I have ever felt. She whispered in my ear, "Thank you." I cried all the way home thinking about it.

***

July Fourth was on a Monday that year. The supervisor had left the week prior for a mission trip, and the shop was ours to do with as we pleased. It was decided the Friday prior to the holiday that we needed a break. After the necessities of trash, bathrooms, and general appearances were performed, we would have an old-fashioned pig roast. We invited all the other area units and by lunch the maintenance yard looked like a convention.

I deliberately stayed sober, enjoying the company, listening to stories I had heard many times before, but mostly to keep a watch on

Edgar. He had consumed most of the two thirty-packs of beer I had brought in before they had a chance to get cold in the ice chest. I waited with a cat's dedication to catch a mouse for him.

Round about five o'clock, all that remained of the pig was gristle and bone. By tomorrow morning, even that would be lost to the raccoons. The men's car keys jingled with drunken delight as they tried to unlock and start their personal and company vehicles alike. Some would stay on the back roads and hopefully get home without killing anybody. Most would crawl into the driver's seat, turn on the radio, and sleep it off here. I had kept myself busy cleaning up paper plates and aluminum cans, waiting until I was certain everyone was either passed out or gone.

Edgar was comatose, sitting at a picnic table, beer still in hand, and with his head lolled back as if deeply interested in astronomy. I came over to him with a fresh beer, the top already open and woke him.

"Edgar!" I yelled and shook him until his eyes opened.

Disorientated he asked, "Wha'…what ja' want?"

"The party ain't over 'til it's over," I said as I put his arm over my back and raised him upright. I set the new beer to his lips. It was like nursing a newborn calf. Nothing much required of me except to let nature take its course.

He belched in my face before he yelled, "Party!"

Without any resistance I led him to my car, taking particular care to fasten his seat belt.

"Safety first," I said to him as he looked questioningly about my concerned actions. It was our company motto. A mantra that we said aloud to each other anytime we had to follow an asinine rule in flagrant disregard for common sense.

Drunkenly, he repeated after me. "Safety first," and promptly fell asleep.

I drove slow and cautious to the rat hole trailer park where he lived. It was common knowledge among the meth set that this place was paradise.

As I unloaded him from the car into the trailer, he popped in and out of consciousness. Finally able to deposit him on to the couch, I went back to get my purse from the trunk. When I came back in, I was shocked to see him sitting up, fully awake, and holding a fresh beer. The kind that was triple the size of a normal can, what my ex called the breakfast of champions.

The can fell to the floor with a thunk, spraying the beer across the arm of the couch. He laughed, giving a half-hearted salute to his fallen comrade. When he looked up at me clutching my purse, his laughter stopped, and that damned smile grew on his face like mold. Edgar loosened the top of his blue jeans and unzipped his fly, exposing himself to me.

"C'mon baby," he said. "If ya didn't want this, ya wouldn't be here."

"Is that what you told Cindy."

I reached in my purse and pulled out the gun.

In a moment he was up. He lunged for me, but his open pants considerably slowed his attack. On his knees, he looked up at me, laughing again as he looked straight into the Beretta's barrel.

"Stupid cunt," he cursed me as I pulled the trigger over and over again.

***

I stared into the twelve pairs of eyes as I finished my story. I couldn't read them. Some were emotionless, some full of empathy, but most were in shock.

I saw Cindy sitting in the gallery, crying quietly into a tissue. Next to her my two boys with my ex. He had been awarded temporary custody pending the outcome of this trial.

Now that I had said everything I could remember, his honor excused me from the stand. I watched the seven women and five men leave to deliberate my judgment, to decide, as I had, on the merit of another human being's intentions. Regardless their decision, I had no regrets.

Good Intentions

I push my way through the double glass doors of Bailey, Taylor, Shipman, Shipman, and Davis. The sign is erroneous, and I make a mental note, as I have every morning for the last nine months, to have the first Shipman removed.

Marvin is currently in the federal slam serving an eight-year sentence. Due to the nature of his crime, he spends twenty-three hours of every day in 'protective custody.' That's code for solitary confinement with television. His amazing mind for jurisprudence trapped, useless and dormant, by the futility that is prison life.

I remember when the feds broke into our offices like boot-heel Nazi thugs. Their automatic weapons drawn as they generally terrorized the shit out of middle-aged secretaries whom hadn't so much as jaywalked in their whole lives.

The leader, a guy dressed in a pin-stripped Brooks Brothers' suit that fit him well fifty pounds ago, handed out the search warrants. He had the foresight to make sure there were enough copies for each of the partners, the associates, and even interns. The warrant was more seizure more than search. They wanted computers, every one Marvin was known to have used at any time, whether at work, home, or otherwise. By the time they left, the only computer that remained belonged to the file clerk.

Marvin was a pedophile. Not the kind grabbing kids from school bus stops, but without guys like him, shit like this would cease to exist. He was charged with the purchase, possession, and distribution of pornographic images of a minor under the age of ten years. To be more succinct: kiddie porn.

His wife of twenty years divorced him before he was sentenced. She took her fifty percent, as prescribed by law, and the court took the remainder to be held in a slush fund called the 'victims reimbursement program.' I suspected it was the cost of doing business. A tax levied upon the offender, guaranteeing his life outside of bars to be so miserable that if he didn't kill himself, he certainly wouldn't be of any significant trouble in the future.

I loved my brother, in spite of what he had done, and faithfully represented him. I was able to get him a plea-bargain, that saved him fifteen years, with the usual caveats. He could never practice law again. He would have to register as a sex offender. He would have to surrender his passport. He couldn't be stopped, standing, or otherwise, within fifteen hundred feet of any school. All standard and reasonable clauses, that was always demanded and completely pointless toward rehabilitation. I wished we could have opted for castration. That, at least, would have been a reasonable solution for everyone involved.

"Morning, Warren," my secretary chimed.

My voice percolated inside my throat. The normal grunt sounds I used to communicate my thoughts when words seemed too troublesome.

She handed me a stack of pink notes, mostly missed calls from clients. One in particular though struck me odd enough to find my voice.

"What in the hell does he want?" I asked myself.

"The call was collect," she said. "I couldn't accept."

Before I could look up from the handwritten script, her fingers were a blur. The plastic keys beneath her glossy red fingernails clacked away at the body of a letter. The small black letters formed on the monitor like stitches in a blanket. I wondered if she even read what she was given to type any longer?

I sat down at my desk and put the note to the side. It could wait. I concentrated on the first rule of law: deal with the paying customers before even thinking about a pro bono client's problems.

After a busy morning of answering client's stupid questions, or as it is sometimes called 'practicing psychiatry without a license,' I finally had time to return my attention to the odd note.

I dialed the number. A ring-tone buzzed through my end of the extension, as if I were making an overseas call and not simple long distance to an isolated, if not forgotten, patch of Missouri farmland called Sikeston.

It took fifteen minutes before I could be connected to the highly controlled extension. I could almost see the plain, beige phone, reminiscent of a rotary, sans the dial. When the automated message played to remind me all conversations would be recorded and reviewed for content, is when I quit daydreaming.

"I was beginning to think you wouldn't call me back," Marvin said cheerfully through the static. You would think I was calling him at his summer place in the Ozarks.

"I'm your attorney," I remind us both. "It's my duty."

"How's Mary?" he asked disregarding my official tone.

"She's fine," I say not willing to engage in small talk at three dollars a minute.

I wait for him to speak. In the background I can clearly hear the sounds of dozen thirteen-inch televisions. It sounds weird, the mixture of news, cartoons, and talk shows. The humdrumity of passing time without hope it would go any faster.

After a full minute, Marvin spoke. "I've got a good one here."

My shock is impossible to disguise. "What the hell are you talking about?"

A 'good one' is an unofficial term for a case not listed in any legal text. It means you've found a case that is winnable and consequently a decent payday. The idea that my brother was still hound dogging for clients gave me a momentary elation. It quickly dissipated when I rationalized he was probably losing his mind.

Without my responding, he elaborated. " A young guy, lives across the hall from me. I've thoroughly interviewed him," he said like he was talking to me from the extension in his old office and not from cell block fourteen. "I am completely convinced he is innocent. Unfortunately, my current situation offers certain restrictions."

"No shit," I blurted. "Jesus, Marvin, everyone there is innocent, ask them." My frustration was diluted by my compassion. To keep from losing his sanity he set up shop in a four by eight foot room of concrete and metal bars. It wouldn't have surprised me if he had somehow had a sign made by the convicts pronouncing him:

Marvin Shipman

Convicted Pervert, Former Attorney at Law

"This boy is different. He doesn't belong here, Warren."

"What's your proof?"

"I can't talk about that on the phone."

"You have got to be…" I dropped off in mid-sentence when something occurred to me. "You don't expect me to come all the way down there, to talk to him myself?"

"Of course I do," he said. "How else will you be able to sign him up?"

The idea of the three and a half-hour drive did not thrill me. To see my brother, I had no problem. I had made it a point to see his time served in the state. His rotting away in some cell a thousand miles from home was not an idea I found comfortable. With the Thanksgiving holiday rolling around things would be slow. It would be a perfect time to make the trek.

"All right," I said, "I'll come take your client's statement."

Marvin was nobody's fool. He was locked up because he had grown sloppy in his habit, like all junkies eventually do, not because he was stupid.

"Look asshole," he attacked me, "I can remember plenty of times I pulled your ass out of the fire. No questions asked. You needed help and I delivered. Should I go into the details of four August, nineteen eighty-eight."

The son of a bitch, I thought, he was prepared to trump my ass with the blackmail card from the beginning.

"Marvin---"

"I would hate to bring to light how on that night, a certain attorney and an underage drinking partner---"

"Enough!" I shouted. I'm sure whoever was listening to this conversation was having a good laugh. It's not often a con has this much control over his lawyer. "I can be there Thursday morning. Is that good enough?"

"That's Thanksgiving."

"It'll give your client a reason to be thankful."

"What about Mary?" he asked.

"Let it go, Marvin," I said hanging up the phone.

***

I left the office early Wednesday afternoon and wished my secretary a happy holiday. In kind she did the same. We exchanged a platonic hug, then I went home to pack.

The house was quiet. I still wasn't accustomed to living alone. Mary had left a year ago last week. My advocacy for Marvin in court, fighting the good fight, pissed her off to the core.

"How can you do this?" she would morosely ask.

Every night of the trial, it was the same thing.

"He's my brother."

"He's a monster and a purveyor of filth. The lowest kind of human being imaginable. Why do you have to do it? There must be somebody else."

"I don't think so."

"Do you realize all the neighbors know? The things they say. Your name, our name, on the front page everyday, airing our dirty laundry."

"I don't give a damn, Mary. He's always been there for me and now it's my turn."

That usually shut her up.

Her arguments with me eventually became unilateral warfare with a bottle of Absolute. Before the trial was over, she had quit talking to me.

The night she wrapped her BMW around a light pole downtown, I had to pull an all nighter. Like a coward, I sent my senior associate to post her bond. At the time it made sense. She knew work always came first. By the time I came home to shave and change into my power suit, a blue Italian job that had cost me more than my first new car, she was gone.

The emptiness of our home didn't affect me until after Marvin's trial. The crystal was still in the cabinet, and the maid service took care of housework. Her scent, though, was gone.

My overnight bag packed, I stopped and stared into the walk-in closet. The room built to hold our clothes was hardly smaller than our first apartment in college. With her half empty, it looked much bigger.

As I prepared to leave, certain the coffeepot timer was off and windows were locked, I noticed the answering machine. The number one flashed, warning me, a message waited to be heard. I pushed the play button. Instantly I recognized Mary's voice.

"Warren, are you home? Please pick up if you're there." Pausing momentarily, she continued as if I was listening. *"Mother wanted me to call and wish you a happy Thanksgiving. She insists on your coming up for dinner Thursday. I've tried to explain how busy you are, that it is hard for you to get away. Still..."* She stopped again. I could tell she was trying to choose her words. *"Look, I don't give a rat's ass one way or the other. Come if you want or don't, but do, please call Mother. This is all very confusing for her, and believe it or not Warren, she loves you and I..."* catching herself in mid-sentence, she edited her usual farewell salutation to me, *"hope you are doing well."*

"I hope you are doing well too," I said aloud, trying the words out for myself. Nothing could ever replace 'I love you,' but it was nice. I played the message again, then erased it.

***

I drove eighty miles an hour on cruise control as soon as I passed the county limits. The straight road offered no challenges and the passing farmland no distraction. By the time I made it to Sikeston, it was dark. From the highway you could see the Wal-Mart sign and the faint square shape of the prison.

The motel was the best the town had to offer. Better than a commercial chain, but by no means a real hotel. I was fairly sure the middle-aged woman who checked me in, swiped my Visa card, and explained to me how to make long-distance calls would be the same person in the morning making my bed, cleaning my toilet, and inspecting my room for its' overall tidiness.

She was nice enough, saying the prison would have amended hours for the holiday. An hour earlier than normal, friends and family would be let in to see the incarcerated.

"What about attorneys?" I asked trying to make a joke.

"A visitor is a visitor, I guess." she said.

I found my room easily enough and slid my key into the gold-plated lock. The solid thump of the dead bolt retreated inside the steel door. What they lacked in amenities they certainly made up for in security. Possibly it was the idea that less than two miles away rapists, murderers, and pedophiles were kept behind bars. Maybe the doors, the locks, and the better-than-average security cameras in the manager's office and on the parking lot gave visitors peace of mind. I thought it all was smoke and mirrors. What better deterrent is there to crime than having a federal penal institution in your backyard?

After I unpacked, I undressed and lay down nude under the clean sheet. The last thing I thought before falling asleep, regardless the bullshit reason my brother had called me down here was that it would be nice to see him.

***

Above the visitors entrance should have hung a sign reading *'abandon all dignity here.'* Men, women, and children were randomly grabbed and prodded by the overtly diligent guards searching for contraband. Christ, with the consistency of these searches, my third thus far, I couldn't imagine the ingenuity by which all the reported drugs were getting in the place.

Like a dumb ass, I had forgotten to leave my Montclair pen back at the hotel. It was gift from a friend whom I had successfully defended against charges of unlawful carnal knowledge. The pen had become a part of my apparel, but I should have thought about it.

I argued to no avail with a guard who practically proved Darwinisim. The huge moron kept repeating the same phrase over and over again. "You may file an incident report for improper seizure with the Warden's office, sir." I figured I would shut-up while I was ahead. If you didn't treat these people with kid gloves, you would be bent over holding your ankles. A BCS (body cavity search) was a thrill I was not hoping to experience any time soon.

The visitor's area; a collection of perfectly spaced round stainless steel tables set permanent into the concrete below them. I looked for Marvin. A sea of orange jump suited men sat one per table as a bullpen of candidates waited and smoked behind what I presumed to be soundproof glass. White men, black men, brown men, and yellow men with less freedom than a damn dog tied to a stake and almost utterly forgotten by the society that placed them here. I still believed that in a truly democratic society of justice, those given life sentences should be allowed the bullet option. That is placed alone in a room with a gun, loaded and cocked, they could make one final free decision. Screw the Eighth Amendment. Until you spend a year in a hellhole like this, stripped of your pride, your culture, your identity as an individual, you have no idea how rational an idea it is.

Among the safety orange prison jumpsuits, Marvin in his lime green stood out. The idea was to easily tell special protection cases from the general population. In essence, make it easier for the testosterone-driven gorillas that ran the place not to accidentally throw him in with the animals. Despite their own atrocities, they would tear him limb from limb.

Escorted to his table, I sat with my legal pad and no pen. I was obliged the loan of what was once a pencil by the humorless guard.

Marvin's salt and pepper hair had gone shock white. He had lost weight and his eyes had taken on perpetual glaze. Older by ten years, he looked more like my father now than my sibling.

"Happy Thanksgiving," he said.

Inside this place it was implausible to discern it as a holiday. It was probably the first we had spent together sitting at the same table since our mother passed away. I dismissed the melancholy moment for substance and got down to business.

"Name of the client?" I asked.

"Prisoner 664568G, Vasquez, Ricky. Alleged sodomy of a minor."

"At this point that would be convicted," I reminded him.

"True enough," he said, "but innocent."

I almost started to argue with him then remembered the exercise in futility we were both carrying out.

"He was a cop, highly decorated. This is all a setup, like me, the conspirators that run this world have prevailed upon another good man. This time, buddy boy, we got them on improper search."

"A technicality?" I moaned. Once convicted, screaming technical foul was no more effective than shooting bottle rockets at a nuclear warhead. An impropriety such as that would have been raised long ago at an indictment hearing.

"It's true, Warren," he said. "A prima facia fact. Their discovery was because the building manager, a so called friend, opened his locker without Mr. Vasquez's express consent, supposedly looking for cigarettes, which by the way he did not find."

I dreaded the answer before I asked. "What was found?"

"Irrelevant. Next question."

"Damn it, Marvin. You aren't a judge, much less a paralegal. Now answer the question."

"A picture."

"Oh, for the love of Pete!"

"Its circumstantial. But for the Polaroid in Mr. Vasquez's locker, there was no proof to the commission of a crime."

"A goddamn Polaroid! They might have well found him in bed with someone. The Supreme Court has upheld the validity of instant photography under the best documents rule, especially in cases of sexual exploitation of a minor. You of all people should know this."

The guard was closely watching us. A visitor did not normally berate the visited. The scrutiny would be laughable under other circumstances.

"Is that all you have?" I said.

"Res Ispa Loquitor."

How original, I thought, quoting law school idioms to me.

"That's the first thing you've said since I've sat down that has made sense. The thing certainly does speak for itself."

I raised my hand to signal the conclusion of my visit to the correctional officer. As I stood, Marvin remained seated. He refused to shake my outstretched hand good-bye, mad as hell with me I presumed for pissing on his so-called case.

***

Safe behind the motel's door, I listened to the news. Before coming back here, I had bought a fifth of Southern and a twelve pack of Bud. The hard alcohol sizzled in my throat in compliment to the ice-cold beer. I wanted to erase my mind, to completely forget the day, yet seemed to dwell even further about it.

It was only a matter of time before he would send me letters explaining everything from who shot JFK to secret messages only he could decipher in dog food commercials. He had been a brilliant man. That was the problem. People like him didn't easily shut down. The mind, desperate for its former activity, created scenarios to fill the void. I felt ashamed. Empathetic. Absolutely hopeless. My personal open bar was the perfect salve.

The instructions next to the phone were blurry, but discernible. In two more beers they wouldn't be. Slow and exact, I followed the simple directions and dialed the number out that I knew as well as my own.

Ready to hang up on the third unanswered ring, a voice, foreign at first, came through the extension.

"Hello? Hello?"

It was like a button had been pushed somewhere inside my brain. I had made this call, obviously I must have wanted to talk, but now the simple words to express myself had become complicated. I regretted the idea the moment my mother-in-law answered instead of Mary.

"Karen," I said knowing damn well it was she, "I need to speak to my wife."

"You're drunk," she said.

I bit my tongue. To call her a bitch, even rightfully so, and demand to speak with Mary would get me nothing but the dial tone. However, she was right about my being drunk, so I was willing to kiss her ass.

"Please, Karen. It has been one hell of a rough day."

The old woman said nothing, allowing me to hang in the breeze. She was thinking it over.

"Happy Thanksgiving, Warren," she said. The phone pounded down on the countertop below where the phone had been installed thirty years ago. I couldn't help but hear her mother yell her daughter's name. Through the receiver I could hear Mary's hurried steps long before she picked up the phone.

"Hello," she said a bit out of breath.

"I'm sorry. Is this a bad time?" I asked not caring.

"No, I heard mother yelling and…quite frankly Warren mother isn't doing so good these days. Thank God it was only the phone."

"Good thing you're there now." I paused trying in vain to put a positive spin on the situation. "I would even venture to say it quite fortuitous you---"

"Warren," she interrupted, "what is it you actually want?"

"Come again?"

"You always do this. Let's skip the foolishness for once."

"I'm in Sikeston." I took a shot down and a quick sip of beer letting the idea sink in for her. The whiskey stung as it slid through my chest. "I miss you," I said.

This kind of drinking was as dangerous as diving head first off a hundred-foot cliff. You could easily remember everything up until the point of the jump. Maybe one, or two things briefly on the way down, then nothing once you hit the water: the welcome, sweet oblivion that was an alcohol blackout.

"You don't miss me," she said, "you miss the idea of me."

"I don't understand," I said slurring my words. Shit, I silently cursed myself. I had hoped not to seem so pathetic. The sincerity by which I placed this call might be dismissed as nothing more than drunk dialing.

"You miss me laying out your clothes and fixing your breakfast. You miss having me to go out to dinner with or attend parties with you, somebody to talk with and sleep next to. I know because I miss those things, too. Your brother was the straw that broke the camel's back."

"What do you want me to do about it?" I asked, my toes gripping the edge of the cliff.

"There's nothing to do but go on."

Ready to defy gravity, I asked, "Do you still love me, Mary?"

"Happy Thanksgiving, Warren," she said as I dove headfirst toward the black water.

After she hung up I remembered holding the phone to my ear dumbly listening to the dial tone. Desperate for attention and more alcohol I drove blind drunk to where I don't know. Then, in fragmented bits and pieces, I could recount loud music and people dancing. Then came the cold, as if I had fallen asleep inside a deep freezer. Finally nothing.

***

I woke back up with the startled fright of a nightmare I couldn't remember or explain. Through the bars I could see a Stetson-wearing sheriff. The dated copy of Maxim held between his hands was well worn and familiar. If he were more than twenty, I would have been surprised. Still, I respected the office he held and recognized the position I was in.

"Excuse me, Sheriff," I called out to him.

He came to at the sound of my voice and shoved the magazine into a drawer. A slight tinge of red colored his cheeks, embarrassed to be caught by a prisoner deficient in his duty. It was an old habit of mine to read the tags of civil servants and always act dumber-than-shit in their presence.

His read, 'D. Boyd'. Above that, in all caps, the inscription 'TRAINEE.' Of course they would put a rookie to watch over the holiday drunk tank. In a town this size, they had maybe four full-time guys and a dispatcher who doubled as janitor.

"Might I trouble you for a cup of coffee?"

The young sheriff stood, squared his shoulders, and adjusted his Wal-mart special belt about his waist. As he sauntered over to the pot, I immediately noticed he did not have a gun.

Through the bars he passed me a Styrofoam cup. I greedily sipped at the hot, black nourishment. It instantly gave me heartburn as it mixed with the acids in my stomach.

He sat back down, not sure what to do with himself. I did my best to ignore him as he aimlessly shuffled papers about the desk to look busy.

I presumed it was five in the morning by the clock hung high enough you would need a stepladder to change the time. In another hour, a regular sheriff would relieve the rookie, and I would be given a full account of the charges against me. I would pay my fine, be released upon my own recognizance, and go home.

Until then, I could think about what I had done.

Humidity

Uncle Casey lost his leg in a motorcycle accident but told everyone he lost it in the first Gulf War. It didn't matter to me, however, it did strike me as unethical for a former policeman to tell such a blatant lie.

I had aspirations of becoming a cop. I thought by working with him that the experience would prove invaluable. It certainly couldn't look bad on my police academy application that I was an assistant private investigator.

So far I had learned PI was synonymous with amateur pornography. My uncle's favorite proverb was "If their pants are down, they're gonna be found." I thought it was stupid, if not inconsiderate, seeing as our specific job was to destroy somebody's life. Curiosity, though, is a dangerous thing. One moment, a person is happy as hell with two cars, a home in the suburbs, and kids who say sir and ma'am. The next, they were sitting in a booth at the Waffle House, crying their eyes out. Uncle Casey with digital pictures by the dozens of the unfaithful spouse playing 'does it fit' with some stranger. Secretly, I believed he took pleasure in watching the whole damned thing unfold.

The pay, though, was terrific. I had friends with degrees busting their chops at jobs, working forty hours or more a week, who struggled to survive. In the year since I dropped out of college and started PI'ing, money became a non-issue. People paid you whatever you said it would take, and Uncle Casey taught me to always get the money in advance. Once you showed the pictures it was game over. If you didn't have the money by then, it wasn't coming.

The hours were an insomniac's dream. On a typical night, we would start to shadow a cheater no earlier than nine and if we were lucky, we were on our way home with the goods by two a.m. Most nights, however, I didn't hit the sack until sunrise.

It could go on as long as three or four days with some of these people. Out of the house to meet their dirty little secret at some secluded destination, to make out like curious teenagers in the back of the family car, then back home to pretend nothing happened. It amazed me we were ever hired. How in the hell could these people not know? Then again, I guess you see what you want to see.

    Somewhere about one in the morning, I was on fumes. Uncle Casey and I sat in his van behind the silver reflective glass that was good for seeing out but not vice versa. Three cameras (one digital, one still, and one streaming video) watched tonight's alleged cheat. He was a middle-aged guy, too fat and too old for the clothes he wore. The woman was half his age, probably somebody he worked with, genuinely smitten with his worldly expertise. A total Daddy fetish if I ever saw one. Sick to death of the whole cat-and-mouse game and tired as hell, I asked Uncle Casey if he wanted some coffee.

    The Coffee Cartel was a few blocks over. It was a gourmet coffee shop modeled off the Seattle wunderkind but without any of the pretension. It was also open twenty-four hours a day, seven days a week. A bastion for students cramming for exams with bottomless refills of dark roast Colombian and free wi-fi. The great thing about coming in at this time of night was no line. Come in here during the morning rush and you were twenty people deep, about to stroke out from a lack of caffeine, and the pressure of being late for work. Lunch was the middle-class housewife hour. Women in their mid-thirties drank coffee for three hours with more sugar than Cap-n-Crunch while they ate diet biscotti. Every night an open mic was available. Bad poetry, odes to angst that made Nirvana lyrics seem happy, pleased the disaffected set. Despite all that, I liked it. The coffee was good and it was always ready.

    This job had been a record six-day crawl. It seemed chicken shit had a complex about an extra-marital exchange of fluids and couldn't pull the trigger. Fine by me. The longer hesitant-Harry wrestled with his conscious, the more money I made.

***

    Tommy was a born rat snitch. If you wanted everyone to know something, all you had to do was tell him. It was no wonder why he wanted to be a cop.

I took him on as a favor to my brother. Him being a one-year community college wash out, working thirds at a local stop-and-rob wasn't a big resume builder. Besides, I could use the company.

I hadn't had a partner since the force. It was a deliberate decision on my part. Partners were a pain in the ass. Before long you were knee deep in their life, whether you wanted to be or not. Generally you only had the job in common, but that didn't stop the chatter. I never married or had kids, but every one of my partners did. The torture of feigning interest in little Johnny's school play or little Susie's dance recital was enough to drive me to drink. Their lives were a scheduled list of things to do. I was overjoyed when I got reassigned to the motorcycle division.

I was more embarrassed than crippled when I dumped my police-issued Harley-Davidson. My leg was no big deal, hell I had two, but the idea that I wasn't in pursuit of some wanted felon is what killed me. That I overcorrected to miss a fucking alley cat totally pissed me off.

After I got out of the hospital, I planted my prosthetic foot in front of the other and decided to hang out my shingle. Money wasn't much motivation. I had plenty with my disability and partial pension. It was the job, the thrill of adult hide-and-seek that motivated me.

I rented an office in Soulard smaller than my bathroom. The rent was triple what it should have been, but I liked the location. A short limp away stood several good taverns that catered to the bored and thirsty at ten in the morning.

I charged clients on a sliding scale. The more I thought they had, the more I charged. Nobody came to me who couldn't afford it. Blue-collar folks didn't have affairs. They fucked around and came home or didn't. Either way, no mystery there.

White collars were an entirely different story. Those people were clueless. With all their money and education you would think they would know better. I heard the same thing so many times it blended into one standard story.

My husband (or wife) recently got that big promotion or some mega-client. I knew the change would be difficult, certainly more hours at the office, but lately things are different. He always seems so preoccupied when he's home. Constantly making phone calls with the bedroom door shut and when I ask, "Who was that dear?" he practically tears my head off. Then there are the meetings in the middle of the night. If I call, I can never reach him. When he comes home, he stinks of cigarettes and liquor. In the morning, before I can ask how things went, he is already telling me that things are going terrible with this new client, and he will probably be stuck in a meeting until late tonight. "Don't wait up," he yells from the driveway without a kiss on the cheek or hug goodbye. Then he is suddenly called out of town. "Unavoidable. I'm the only one who can go, dear. Do you want me to stay home and lose my job?" No, of course not, but why the sudden urgency? I'm not the suspicious type, and I know this will be money wasted, but I HAVE TO KNOW.

That's it in a nutshell, the four magic words that give me carte blanche to dig deeper than a grave robber at midnight. I would like to tell you I have been surprised on occasion. That Mr. CEO or Mrs. Powersuit was putting together a gagillion dollar merger to conquer the world and secure a golden parachute for retirement by age fifty-five. Maybe they were, but the camera doesn't lie.

I always choose a public place to show them the pics. The atmosphere of the Waffle House is best. I order coffee and tip the waitress early to leave us be.

Then the damnedest thing always happens. After the shock turns to numbness, after the wronged party realizes the horrible facts at hand, they say, "Thank you." It never fails. The first time it happened I wanted to scream, but the more it happened the less it began to effect me. Now I have to control the urge to laugh.

I had my doubts at first about Tommy. He felt more compassion for the clients than I liked. He was always wondering who they were and why they would do this? They had everything life could offer.

I was careful to never refer to anyone by name around him. Instead I would use some iconic figure from bad television to identify the targets. It unnerved the kid and gave me a hobby. I would say, "Looks as if Mrs. Brady loves Sam the butcher's meat," or "Ward sure is teaching the Beaver a lesson tonight." Eventually, he quit asking stupid questions.

***

  I've worked at the Coffee Cartel for the last eight months. The money sucks but the fringe benefit of all the free coffee I can drink can't be beat. My personal favorite is the extra strong Ethiopian blend. It's like swallowing raw nuclear energy.

  I have to wear a uniform, but beyond that my appearance isn't taken seriously. Black lipstick and nail polish are essentials for me. Since I started, my hair has been blue, green, and a brilliant pink cut into a bob. In a place like this, I hardly get noticed. My manager has a Mohawk, and the other girl keeps her head shaved to display an intricate array of tribal tattoos.

  The continual infusion of caffeine into my system also helps me to keep from crashing. On average, I sleep five hours max. My time outside of here is a never-ending pursuit for methamphetamine. As a kid, my mother was hooked on what she called trucker diet pills. When she got clean, she ballooned from a hundred twenty-five pounds soaking wet to over two-fifty. The woman who used to move at the speed of light now puttered along in agony. Sobriety seemed an unfair trade of bad for worse.

  Now that I had the habit, I had no plans to ever quit. My friend, Reggie has snorted so much meth she burnt out her sinus passages. She has lost the ability to taste anything. She could be fed a shit-filled sandwich and it wouldn't matter. Her nose is a sieve constantly oozing a clear mucus tide that doctors say can't be fixed. She always has a crumpled hand-full of wet tissues trying to contain the mess, but that is not her biggest sorrow in life. Her chief complaint is that she cannot snort it anymore. I mean she's tried like hell, but it gets all caught up in that gooey mess and none of it goes down. There ain't nothing sadder than a junkie sitting on a mound of their favorite chemical and unable to use. She has to inject it to get high now. I'm certain it'll be the death of her. It's just a matter of time. If an accidental overdose don't kill her, then a dirty needle will.

  My work certainly doesn't suffer any from my addiction. I recently made employee-of-the-month due to my 'outstanding work ethic.' Shortly after that, the day-shift manager offered me a sunshine slot. I thought seriously about it. The money was better for sure and I could probably triple my tips. On the other hand, I wasn't the greatest people person. The zombies I served now were my kind of freaks. People who talked little and asked for less in the way of friendly service. Take the money, give them the coffee, and they went away. No one ever complained.

The day shift was an epidemic of clean smelling, wide-eyed coffee elitists. When I first walked in here to fill out an app, I heard this: "I want a tall, half-skinny extra hot split quad shot latte, hold the whip." I almost walked out. What the hell happened to, "Give me a coffee to go?" That's why I liked the night shift. Nobody gave a shit. If you were in here between twelve and six, your only goal was to keep awake.

When the clean-cut republican came in for the sixth night in a row, I knew he wanted to talk. Typically, no one came in here to stay without a book, a computer, or a friend. After I served him two Turkish Vente dark roasts, I turned my back on him and pretended to wipe down my station. When I turned around and saw him still there, I felt trapped. I gave him his goddamn coffee, what more did he want?

"Can I help you, sir?" I asked with as much derisiveness as I could muster.

"You're name is Jenny," he said.

"Congratulations. You can read."

"I'm Tommy."

"Good for you."

He continued to stand there, not ready to leave, and not certain if he should try again.

"I'm not interested," I said.

"Interested in what?'

"You."

"How did you---"

"It's one o'clock in the morning. If you're not pimping for Jesus or trying to sign me up to vote, then what's left?"

"You're right," he said. A cup of coffee in each hand, he used his back to push open the door. I watched him until the sticky, black night swallowed him whole.

He reminded me of a boy, the first boy, I had kissed. Maybe that's why I had been so mean toward him. Then again, maybe I was too strung out to know good from bad any longer. Christ, I thought, at this rate it was a matter of time before I would be completely delusional.

Ademption

Father Gabriel walked down the hallway mumbling to himself and moving fast. He had been Mike's coach in everything from baseball and girls to picking a college. Father Gabriel was a good guy, one of the few men who didn't take shortcuts. A man like his father.

Mike had deliberately opened a small law office about an eight-hour drive from home. He and his partner were both sons of prominent men. Mike's father had been the unopposed Jefferson County Sheriff for the last thirty years. Chad, Mike's partner, had it even worse. His father, who had been an attorney, was now an appellate court judge.

Their office did mainly small stuff: speeding tickets, community service commitments and simple contract work. Mostly, they gave more advice away over the phone than they charged for in their shared office. Maybe later, when they had wives and kids, they would become more like their fathers. Until then they would leave the mess of saving the world to better men.

The phone was already ringing as he unlocked the office door and took off his light jacket. The slow, mystical fireworks celebration called fall was about to turn the leaves red and orange.

Mike ignored the phone and turned on the coffeepot. The coffmaker's drip triggered a Pavlov reaction in him to urinate. He resisted. The phone kept ringing.

The phone's aggravating, modern bleep made him melancholy for a real bell. The only time you heard bells anymore was on Sunday, but even those were recordings.

In a quick exchange, Mike stole a half-cup of the still brewing coffee. He sat at his desk blowing away the top layer of heat. Eager to take his first sip, he watched the phone. By now, a rational person would have hung up and called another office. It was a small town, but hell, there was more than one lawyer to be had.

"Law offices," he answered trying to sound as disinterested as possible.

"Mike, it's Mom," she said identifying herself as she always did. Must be something to do with her generation. Chad said his mother did the same damn thing every time she called too.

"It's your dad, Mike," she said. Her voice was hoarse, and it sounded like she was trying not to cry. "There's a tumor. He has cancer."

The wind rushed out of Mike's lungs. It was by the barest amount of oxygen he could still breathe.

"There's nothing that can be done but make him comfortable," she said. Her words, emotionless and rehearsed, but still potent.

Mike gripped the phone tightly, as if letting go meant falling into a deep pit. He felt dizzy.

"How…long?" Mike asked, the simple question hard to enunciate.

There was a pause. He could hear his Mother holding the hospital payphone away, blowing into her Kleenex, and trying to keep her composure. He was in no rush for her to give him an answer.

"Three weeks at most," she said, then asked, "How soon can you come home, Mike?"

When Chad came in, he told him the bad news and that he didn't know when he would be coming back. They shook hands and then hugged. Before lunch, he was on the road.

***

He drove all night thinking about how quickly life changed. The idea that a man as vibrant as his father could suddenly be dying angered him.

His father's whole life had been in the service to others. Trivial ideas of retirement, hunting and fishing as the seasons afforded themselves, golfing for the hell of it on a Wednesday morning, were gone. As painful as the thought of his mother being alone was, the reality he believed would be a thousand times worse.

On the phone his mother had said they had discovered Father in a closed flea market a hundred miles from home. Later, they found his truck in a ditch, still in drive and the engine running.

The owner had come upon him while picking up litter. By the cuts on his hands and his torn clothes, it was obvious he had climbed over the barbed-wired fence. The owner asked him what did he think he was doing there? Mike's father said he didn't know. When he told him he better get out, he didn't move. The owner said he was going to call the police. When he still didn't move, he did exactly that.

The police came, and like the owner, asked him the same things. Again, he said he didn't know. They asked him for his name. For a moment he stared at them, seeming not able to understand their question. His mind was a freshly cleaned blackboard. The indecipherable faded chalk lines that used to be knowledge now meant nothing to him. Then, he told them the only thing he could. "I don't know."

The police asked him to stand to be searched and he automatically complied. The younger officer pulled a billfold from Father's back pocket and handed it to the older cop. When he opened it and found a gold badge along with his drivers' license, they ceased their interrogation and called for an ambulance.

In the hospital the standard tests were conducted. The man was the epitome of physical fitness. It wasn't until the MRI machine revealed an egg-sized black mass above his spine that a diagnosis was made.

It was inoperable, malignant, and would turn him into a vegetable shortly before it killed him. The tumor had been growing for at least the last three to four years. Even if, by some miracle, it would have been found back then, aggressively combated with chemo and radiation, the odds of him living much longer than he already had weren't any better.

Mother had asked Mike to come specifically to help. She would be by Father's bedside from six in the morning till six at night, then Father's brother Henry would be there until eleven. Mike's shift would be those uncomfortable hours of total darkness, allowing his mother and uncle to rest. It was a vigil to be enforced without excuse.

A litany of comfort meds kept Mike's father mainly unconscious at least four out of every six hours. When he awoke it was anybody's guess if he would be lucid or hydrophobic. The doctors said that as the tumor progressed, an induced coma would be necessary due to the pain. Until then, they could have him, if only occasionally.

***

He had found Mother as he had expected. Perched silent next to Father in a semi-comfortable hospital chair. She held his hand and looked lovingly, hopefully at the man she loved.

They married the day after he had graduated from the St. Louis Police Academy. After a short stint with city law enforcement and quite possibly by divine providence, he became the new under-sheriff in rural Jefferson County. A year later, the old boy he answered to died of a major heart attack in an Illinois brothel. Youth, integrity, and charm got voters to elect him Sheriff the first time. His vigilance for keeping the peace year after year got him re-elected.

The area had risen up since Father began. He liked to say that they may have the same problems of a big city, but they still had small town values. By that he meant, he still called men older than him sir and expected the same of men younger than him (damn their rank). When the food pantry was asking for donations, you raided the cabinets. Men held doors open for women and waited their turn. It was a nice way to live.

Mike kissed Mother on the cheek. She was happy to see him and knew Father would be pleased with him as well. As he stood next to her, Mike placed his hand over theirs.

"Have you eaten, Mike?" Mother asked.

"A little. Some burgers, a few gas-station hot dogs. Mostly just coffee."

"Go home. Take a shower. Fix yourself something from the icebox," she ordered maternally. "There's more food going to rot in there than is going to get eaten. Then get some rest. Uncle Henry needs you to be here on time."

"Yes, Mother," Mike said kissing her cheek again.

Father hadn't moved except for his deep breaths. A tube went to his stomach that pumped in a nutritional mush. Another, thankfully hidden beneath the hospital blankets, collected his waste.

The prone body was his Fathers, but without the towering six-foot-six frame erect and his 'aw, shucks' smile, he looked different. Not like he was sleeping or deceased, more empty than anything. As if his soul was wandering confused, far away from his body, not entirely certain it should come back to visit.

***

Mike came to the hospital quarter after ten. He had disobeyed his mother's order to go directly home and raided the meager resources of the local Library. He blindly pulled books until he had collected a full armload from the shelves. Some he knew by author, others he chose solely by their cover. The librarian seemed frustrated to be checking out so many books at once. He tried to reassure her using his best imitation of Father's smile. She had no use for such conveyances.

Uncle Henry sat where Mother had been before when Mike came into the room. Unlike Mother, however, his uncle had his boots propped up on the bed, watching the Rams offensive line get trounced by the visiting Forty-Niners.

He bounced to his feet upon seeing his nephew and gave him an unusually long hug. The big man pushed away first. He was a five-year younger carbon copy of Father and seemed all to ready to cry. He changed the subject to avoid it.

"Dang, boy! I ain't seen you since Cindy got married. How's life down there in the middle of God's country?"

"Pretty good. The village has three horses now, but there is talk of getting a fourth."

"Why do all good lawyers have to be such smarty pants?" Uncle Henry asked loving every minute. Mike may have looked like his Mother, but it was a disguise. Inside, he was every bit quick as his father.

Not much for small talk, Uncle Henry shook his nephew's hand and wished him well, then left.

In the still warm chair, Mike sat next to his Father. With nothing to distract him, he randomly chose one of the books he had brought. The story was vaguely familiar and it was likely he had already read it years ago. It offered him a comfort, an escape, he gladly accepted to defy reality.

***

At one a.m., a nurse came into the room. She smiled toward him and wordlessly changed Father's IV's. Methodically, she charted her duties on an aluminum clipboard. Mike was grateful for her silence.

This was the hospice ward. The patients cared for here were not going to become well. The staff and the families who shared these sanitary rooms moved among each other with delicacy. No one wanted to be here but made the best of things if they had to be.

Mike's head was bobbing up and down, trying to resist the natural urge to sleep, when Father awoke.

"What the hell is going on here?" his Father's voice barked.

"Dad," Mike answered.

"I asked a question, boy, and I expect an answer."

The stern response made Mike wonder.

"You're in the hospital, Dad. Mother will be here soon," he said.

"Don't you hand me that hogwash," Father said. "You're in a heap of trouble."

The agitation caught Mike off-guard. He was accustomed to the soft-spoken, laconic man his father normally was.

"Now if you're smart, you'll tell me the truth. I'll do everything I can to make it look good that you confessed."

His Father was awake, but not in the present. Not knowing what else to do, Mike decided he would try and play along.

"I don't know what you're talking about, Sheriff."

"The hell you say."

This game wasn't fun. His Father had helped him a few times with advice on interviewing clients. How to discern the truth from the lies, the facts and not the feelings, no matter what the alleged crime.

He recognized this as a rudimentary backseat-interrogation, some ghost of Christmas past come to visit. Whoever Father was speaking to, he had them dead to rights. In a blatant disregard to his own best advice to clients, Mike confessed.

"You got me Sheriff," Mike said. His intonation reminded him of a black-and-white cowboy movie, maybe something staring Gary Cooper or Henry Fonda. "I'll be happy to oblige you and show you where the gold is buried."

The rage that poured from his Father was a volcanic fount. His face became red, enraged by the obvious insolence. "Son-of-a-whore! Son-of-a-bitch!"

Father's words struck out and felt cold against his cheeks. It was as if he had stepped into an unexpected winter storm. His face burned with shame.

"After what you have done, you're in no position to play games," Father said.

Above a whisper, he answered him in a voice he hadn't used since he lived under the man's roof. "Yes, sir."

"Good," Father said. His rage seemed to have left him as quickly and suddenly as it had found him. He was still mad, but the meds were doing their job. Unable to differentiate pain from outrage, the crystalline water dripped faster into him, releasing its magic formula. "Now, let's start over. Where is…the…girl?"

"What girl?" Mike asked. He asked again shaking Father by his softened bicep, "What girl, Dad?"

His spirit dwelled somewhere else again, far away, waiting.

Mike, now wide-awake, sat with great attention toward Father. The man never discussed his work with him, even after law school. Now he was walking down a nightmare version of memory lane holding his father's hand and praying to God for the strength to continue.

***

His mother came into the room promptly at six. She took pride in being on time and likened tardiness to sin itself. Mike hadn't been less than fifteen minutes early for an appointment, meeting, or casual party since puberty.

"Right on time," Mike said rising to salute Mother with a ritual kiss upon her cheek.

Her focus was immediately drawn toward Father. The machines that surrounded his bedside clicked and beeped with their electronic efficiencies. Mother studied them for the smallest changes. Whether good or bad she wanted to know. Every moment at this point was precious.

"Did he talk to you last night?" she asked as she sat in the chair.

The question surprised Mike. "He did, a little."

"He talked to me yesterday," she said. "He thought we were getting married. I think he is remembering all the good things."

Mike didn't know about that. Mother had been with Father every day for the last thirty-five years. It was no surprise to him there could be a surplus of good memories for her. How couldn't there be? He, on the other hand, had not been making much time for Father since college. Over the last five years, he saw him purposefully two days a year: Fourth of July and Christmas. Beyond that, they talked mildly on the phone. Outside the subject of law, they didn't have much to discuss.

"Will you stay for breakfast?" Mother asked.

Her question brought him back to the present. "Yeah, sure, Mom," he said.

As the day nurse came on, talking with Mother while simultaneously administering to all of Father's needs, he had a thought.

After breakfast he would forego sleep a bit longer. An old friend, an under-grad in pre-law until his senior year, was now a newspaper editor. Maybe he could help him figure out this puzzle.

***

Daniel worked for *The Riverfront Times*, a weekly rag supported mainly by advertisements for strip clubs and bars that were handed out free to the public. Occasionally it broke a real news story.

In the world of journalism, it was a by-line for Daniel, something that would look good on his resume in retrospect. In reality, it was nothing more than a regular paycheck.

Mike had hoped to catch him at the office. After leaving three voice-mail messages, he was almost asleep when Daniel returned his call. Shaking off the cobwebs, they agreed to meet for a late lunch downtown.

After the waitress with a purposefully exposed cleavage left them alone to eat their toasted ravioli and pizza, they were able to talk.

"Sorry about your dad," Daniel said through a mouthful deep fried pasta.

"Shit happens," Mike said. He took a slice from the pizza, but had lost his appetite. "I need you to help me with something, if you can."

"Yeah, man. Anything."

"I'm not sure if this is legit."

"Where I work, that's our specialty."

"I want to know if you can find out about a case my Dad would have worked. It's probably nothing and I doubt you will find anything."

"So what," Daniel said as he let out a smelly belch. "I spend most of my day going over copy written by amateurs that wouldn't be taken seriously by a comic book publisher. I'll run your dad through all the databases. You would be surprised. We all leave digital footprints. Things you wouldn't have thought anybody could know are somewhere. It's a matter of looking in the right place."

"Thanks, Dan," Mike said.

"Your dad was a great sheriff. I'm sure I'll find a ton of stuff."

Mike almost corrected his friend then stopped himself. His use of the past tense in reference to his father was not that far from wrong.

***

Mike was barely able to get four hours of sleep before his shift. After a quick shower, he threw on jeans and a t-shirt despite the cool northerner coming in. The light jacket that had seemed overkill a couple days before now couldn't keep him warm.

Quickly walking into the hospital room, worried he was late, he felt little relief in arriving ten minutes early.

"Sorry", Mike said trying to apologize. "I overslept."

Uncle Henry was once again kicked back with his boots on the bed. He was reading one of the books Mike had brought with him last night. A paperback Mike had grabbed without much thought from the 'Oprah' section about two brothers who sell knives door-to-door for a living. Hell, if she liked it, there was fifty-fifty shot he might as well.

Dog-earing the page to mark his place, Uncle Henry looked his nephew over.

"It's dang near winter, fella. Where's your coat?"

"How's Dad doing?"

"No change."

Mike wanted to know more.

"Did he say anything?"

"Oh, sure," Uncle Henry said falsely, "he said if you see that know-it-all boy of mine, tell him to get a coat from my closet."

"Funny," Mike said, "you should take that act on the road."

"Believe I will," Uncle Henry said. While he put on his coat, he kept hold of the book, shoving it through the sleeve. The pages curled into a thick half-circle. Its cover was now misshapen and creased. Mike almost laughed aloud thinking about how distraught the librarian would be at seeing this.

"Mind if I hang on to this?" Uncle Henry asked waving the book.

"Might as well."

After he gave his uncle a playful bear-hug goodnight, he took over in the chair. Five minutes into his shift, Mike fell asleep.

***

Mike awoke with a start. He didn't realize how tired he truly had been. Mad at himself for it, he reconciled his thoughts of inadequacy by vowing to not allow it happen again.

Father was awake, staring at him. His mouth clamped tight, almost in a grimace, his jaw moved left-to-right as he ground his teeth.

"Dad," Mike said blinking and rubbing his sleep-swelled eyes, "It was an accident. It won't happen again. I promise."

Father's jaw unlocked with a viciousness.

"You'll burn in hell for this, you lousy son-of-a-bitch. I don't give a good goddamn who your family knows up there in Jeff City or how much money they have."

Tonight, Mike promised himself, he would not play games. He wanted answers. If Father was trying to send him a message, it was his duty to decipher the code.

"What is it? Who do you think I am?"

"Don't act stupid. Maybe most folks around here don't give a rat's ass about some little colored girl, but I do. I already called the sheriff and told him what I know you've done. He said he'd be here soon enough. Until then, I'm not to let you out of my sight." The exertion of speaking tired him more than a ten-mile run. Father carefully chose his next words. "I hope the sheriff let's me cut your balls off."

Exhausted, his eyes fluttered closed.

Mike hadn't liked what father had said, but was glad he was consistent. Any doubts he had as to his father's sanity were disqualified. He was of sound mind if only it was in a distant memory.

***

Mother brought Mike a coat, one of Father's many and insisted he put it on before leaving the hospital room. It was a full size to big, accustomed to wider shoulders and a larger tummy. The furry lamb's wool lining dyed dark blue was warm and soft. Two silver rings, where a badge would have been clipped over the left breast, were vacant. He felt like a child playing dress-up.

After breakfast with Mother, he came home. Daniel's voice echoed from the answering machine as he came through the door. He rushed to pick-up the cordless extension, tripped, and fell in a slide across the linoleum kitchen floor. Embarrassed, he used the counter's ledge to get back to his feet.

With regret, Mike pressed the machine's play button. Where his mother loathed tardiness, he hated voice mail, forced to listen to people as they pretended to talk to the person they had called. It seemed counterintuitive. Likewise, he shunned cell phones. How the world's problems were going to somehow be solved while driving seventy miles per-hour was a mystery to him.

"Hey, Mike it's Dan. You there, buddy?" Daniel asked igniting another pet peeve of Mike's. It was like writing a letter with the opening sentence asking if you were reading this. Some things were apparent. "Guess not. Look, dude I've been checking sources against what you told me, but haven't found anything that sits on all four legs. I'm on my way now to meet a buddy. He's got stuff going back before the bible. I've got a hell of a busy day ahead of me. Call me on my cellie if you want, but that's pretty much it for now. I will be in the office all day tomorrow fact-checking. Let's have a couple of brewhahas for old time sake, say about six at Fred's place tomorrow night? Anyway, call me, dude. Let me know what's up."

The machine's feminine-like robot voice announced 'end of message.' Mike stood, thinking things over. Maybe he was chasing shadows in the dark. Daniel said he had nothing. Possibly there was nothing to find after all. Sometimes clients got like this. Regardless what you did for them, you cannot make the facts change. If Daniel found nothing by tomorrow night, he resigned himself to accept that this thing with his father was nothing more than a drug-induced fiction.

***

Mike got a good days rest. When he awoke, Mother had readied a meal fit for a king. Fresh garden-picked salad with homemade Italian dressing, handmade sourdough rolls, deep-fried steak cutlets, home cut fries, and green beans with squares thick as scrabble tiles of maple-cured bacon. It was far from a calorie conscious meal, but it was certainly food for the soul. The comfort of each bite more pleasing than the last.

After supper, he had a cigarette. The smoke helped digest the rich foods and made room for desert. Homemade Brown Betty buried under vanilla ice cream.

"Your father used to smoke. Did you know that?"

"No," Mike said honestly surprised. He never knew of Father having any vices outside of working too much.

"Before you were born, him and his brothers would get together every Sunday. They were all married by then too. We wives would come together in the kitchen frying up chicken and drinking schnapps. The men would be out in the field, shooting targets off the fence line, in between drinks of mason-jar liquor. By the time supper was ready, the whole gang of us were in one hell of a great mood. It would be well after midnight before we would get to bed."

Mike listened serenely to the story. He never thought much about his parents as people. The idea that they were young once was intriguing.

"As soon as I found out I was pregnant with you, I took the pledge. Your father, the consummate gentleman, jumped on the wagon right along with me. Nine months later, you were the center of the universe to us. It wasn't until your first birthday either of us realized we hadn't had a drop in nearly two years. I guess we lost our taste for it. Daddy, though, loved those cigarettes. He got the habit in the service. When we met up, everybody smoked except for me, but it never bothered me one way or another. It was when you were five he quit. Seems you wanted to be like him so bad that you took to picking his butts out of the ashtray, pretending to smoke. That broke his heart."

It made Mike think as he crushed out his cigarette. He had the habit and couldn't conceive life without them. The idea that he had been unwittingly imitating his father made him smile. It was weird, especially at a time like this he thought, the things children found in common with their parents.

"He must've gained forty pounds quitting, but he did it. I thought his new pot-belly was sexy."

Mike laughed out loud more from embarrassment than humor.

"Jesus, Mike," Mother said as her jovial mood turned sullen, "I am going to miss that man so much."

He leapt from around the table and he held his weeping mother's head against his chest. Doing his best to comfort her, he couldn't keep back his own tears.

"Me, too," he whispered resting his cheek on top his mother's head.

***

Father was resting comfortably as the new nurse came in tonight. She was much taller and thinner than the other one, but they had identical smiles. Lips pressed together, raised slightly at the corners, and completely anonymous regarding emotion. It was a smile that said nothing, yet somehow reassured family members.

His uncle seemed more tired tonight. His usual lively banter had taken a more somber appeal, like jokes without punch lines. Father had experienced a couple of serious tachycardia incidents on his shift. The closeness of his brother's waning mortality touched a deeply impacted nerve in the man.

So far tonight on Mike's shift, all was quiet. The steady rhythm of breathing, the regular measurement of heartbeats accented by the chirps of the ever-watchful equipment was almost lulling. It was business as usual and he could have not been more grateful.

At a quarter of five, Father came awake with a yawn. A rested man, seemingly invigorated by a good night's sleep, but groggy absent his ritual coffee. Using a Post-It note to bookmark his place, Mike smiled, glad to see the man he remembered.

"Morning, Dad," Mike said. "How do you feel?"

"How do I feel," he said reiterating the question as philosophy. "I feel sick to my stomach."

"I'll ring the nurse. It's probably the new medicine."

"You got an answer for everything, don't ya?"

The statement made Mike cringe.

"You were never anywhere near the Mopkin's place. From eight p.m. until the following morning, you and Minnie Porter were snug as two bugs in a rug. All evening watching TV with her folks, then spending the night over there due to the storm. Quite the airtight alibi if I do say so myself."

Would this goddamn one-man play never stop, Mike thought.

"Maybe the sheriff is more than willing to swallow that ol' horseshit story, but I'm not. I don't need a new Cadillac nor do I owe a heap of back taxes on my land. I wouldn't give a shit if my family had to live out on the streets if it meant having to take your dirty money.

The truth be told, I can't prove nothing, but if it takes me my whole life, I swear I'll show folks. I don't know how, but I will. No matter who you get to cheat, lie or steal for you, I won't rest until the whole world knows that Rodney David MacArthur II is nothing but a child-murdering rapist not fit to walk the streets. I hope when folks know, they pull you from limb-to-limb and beat you with the bloody stumps. That they drag your Daddy from that big house he bought by selling whores and blackmailing the men who used them and let him watch you die like a dog in the street. Let him see it all and then burn that goddamn mansion of his to the ground with him in it."

Stunned, Mike could not speak or so much as swallow to quench his dry throat.

"I suggest you pack your bags. Leave town before sunset tonight. If you don't, my brothers and I are going to find you. When we do, we'll skin you alive and feed you to the sows. That's a promise, not a threat." His eyes fluttered as the exhaustion grabbed hold of Father once more. In a voice suddenly present and desperate, he weakly reached for Mike's hand, asking, "Do you understand?"

"Yes, Dad," Mike said as the life in his father's eyes retreated from his body again.

It was a secret code after all. Written in a language from one lawman to another. All his life, his father made light of his work. Speeders, drunks, and the Saturday night fights were his only claims to jurisprudence. He should have known better. All men, should they live long enough, have regrets. Should they liver even longer, they might have a chance to absolve the past by preparing for the future.

***

At 9:04 a.m., with Uncle Henry, Mother, and Mike gathered at his bedside, Father gently found his eternal rest. They had loved him the greatest that another person could and he in return shared the same with each of them, every moment of everyday.

***

Father Gabriel gave his father's eulogy and conducted a service fit more for a president than a humble county sheriff. No man could have hoped for more.

At the wake, amongst the dozens of law enforcement officials, Father Gabriel found Mike. He had left the receiving line, his right hand numb from condolences. The priest placed a hand on Mike's knee as he sat in the folding chair next to him.

"I've made a decision Father Gabe," Mike said.

"Times such as these do that to a man."

"The District Attorney is looking for a good prosecutor. I think I'm the man for the job."

"A man who follows his heart can never go wrong," Father Gabriel said. "Of course, there isn't much money in that line of work. It's more a calling than a job, but you know that already, don't you?"

"If my father taught me one thing," Mike said placing his hand over Father Gabriel's "is that money is the least important thing of all."

Take It Or Leave It

The alarm clock woke me at one-thirty in the morning. I slammed my hand in the dark trying my damnedest to silence the hellish screech. Unable to put a stop to the annoyance, I became fully awake and turned on the lamp. The red illuminated digits peered at me from the floor. My vision still blurry made it impossible to clearly see the numbers. I deliberately stomped on it, finally shutting it up before stepping into the john to piss. Pee hit the bowl, the seat, and the floor. A motherfucker of a hangover squealed inside my brain, lending me no mercy for my bad habits.

I brushed my teeth with Listerine, taking the scum off that had built up from cigarettes and beer before passing out. It was the same thing every morning, seven days a week. I spat the brown liquid down the drain followed by a large hunk of lung cheese.

The man I saw in the mirror hadn't changed; a scrubby three-day growth of beard, hair short enough that it was unnecessary to comb, and two bloodshot red eyes with black dots that didn't seem to see anything. I would shower after I got home. My hygiene wasn't an issue. I worked alone.

The clothes I wore were simple. Cargo shorts and a t-shirt during the dog days of summer. Blue jeans and thermal shirts in the winter. Regardless the weather, I wore the same twenty-dollar boots everyday for the last three years. I found the ankle high constriction comfortable. In the slam they made you wear these blue canvas loafers with all white rubber soles. Fifteen years of wearing those goddamn things built a great aversion within me for comfortable footwear. Every time I put my boots on the image of those shoes flashed in my mind until I pulled the laces tight.

It was a cool morning for mid-June but not enough for a jacket. I kept one behind the seat in the van but couldn't remember the last time I used it. I lit a Marlboro and turned the motor over. The piece of shit had an exhaust leak that made a hell of a racket. I punched the accelerator, deliberately revving the engine loud on the apartment's parking lot. All fucking day I listened to screaming kids, the boom-

boom car systems, and people who seemed never to go have to work in order to pay their rent. It was a childish revenge, and I laughed every time. Maybe it didn't bother anyone, but then again, maybe it did. I hoped it pissed somebody off.

I had spent three months living in men's shelters looking for work after my release. The line on the application where it asked if you had ever been convicted of a felony and if so why was easy to answer. With a bold mark, I checked the yes box, and in the space provided wrote one word: manslaughter. If that didn't answer the fucking question, I didn't know what else to say.

Occasionally, I would get an interview in spite of my honesty. Like some kind of asshole, I would wear a long-sleeved shirt and tie that I had picked out of the donation bins, trying to make a good impression. In an instant, before I had even sat down or shook a hand, they all judged me. My only visible tats were across my knuckles that read survivor when put together and the ones on my cheeks. Those were always the kiss of death. In spite of the fact that I was not a racist, anti-Semite, or atheist, the swastika on my right cheek and the upside-down cross on my left made an impact. It wasn't like I couldn't understand. If the roles were reversed, I think I probably would have felt the same way about me. It wasn't until I bumped into an old cellie at a used bookstore downtown that I heard about this gig.

***

Cave was a cool dude, who did his time without incident. In the three years we bunked together, we never had a problem with each other. I hadn't thought much about him since he got early parole for a rape he swore he never committed. Even then, I didn't really give a fuck if he was innocent but got him wise real fast to quit saying that shit. Nothing pissed off locked-down cons than someone screaming injustice at the top of his lungs. Unless he enjoyed getting stabbed with sharpened toothbrushes, I advised him to let it go. If anything, brag about how you did it, and would do it again if they were stupid enough to let you out. He took my advice and suffered a couple of beat downs, which were inevitable once in a while to everybody.

He laughed when I told him how fucked up things had been going. I laughed too. Seriously, what should I have expected? That's when he hipped me to this paper route gig. He explained to me that it was good bread and steady as the sun coming up in the East. The big bonus though was no one gave a shit what you looked like as long as you did your job.

Cave vouched for me to his boss Balentine that night and to my surprise he called me in for an interview. I could tell from the jump that he was not to be fucked with. "Cave says you're a good man. Personally, I don't give a shit what you did. The bottom line is I got enough problems to fill fucking Busch stadium, and I don't need another. This is simple work, but it ain't easy. I expect you to throw papers sick, tired, high, or drunk. They print the paper every day, including Christmas. You miss a day of work, you don't get paid. You miss two in a row and you're fired. I pay every week in cash. It ain't a hell of a lot, but it'll keep you from starving and going homeless. I'll give you a van to use. If you wreck it, I'll shitcan you even if it's not your fault. Steal it, I'll hunt you down like a dog and make you regret the day you were born. I've had guys delivering the paper with IQs lower than a dog's, and they did okay. If all that don't bother you then you can start tonight."

Balentine was right. The job was simple. It only took me a couple of nights to catch on to the routine. A three-ring binder with laminated pages listed the streets, the order in which to drive them, and who got the paper. Balentine changed my route every six months, each one better and usually bigger than the last. I had started in the worst neighborhoods that North St. Louis had to offer. My van had been shot at twice, but it didn't disrupt me from my appointed duties.

That first year, I don't think anything short of the Second Coming of Christ would have stopped me. I liked what I was doing and the punk-ass hoods trying to look all bad weren't shit to the real criminals I had spent almost half my life with in bullpen showers.

The guys who delivered turned over somewhat regular. Cave, a handful of others, and myself were the exception to that rule. Most drivers couldn't make three months in a row. Consequently good drivers were rewarded with the premium routes. Places we couldn't walk through in the light of day we drove through in the bleakest hours. It was my good fortune to have recently been given the Webster run. It was an increase by seventy bucks a week with fourteen hundred papers to throw. I felt like I had won the lottery.

I pulled into the hardware store's parking lot, two vans behind Cave and seventh in the serpentine line. It was a quarter after two and if we were lucky the delivery truck would come before three. No matter what time the asshole driver arrived from the depot, Balentine wanted the papers delivered by no later than six. I never had a problem with that.

The vans were a mix-mosh of pathetic beaters and extravagant custom jobs. Likewise, there were two kinds of carriers. Guys like me who did all the shit work for hard asses like Balentine and the independents. I envied the indies with all the enthusiasm homely girls looked at models in magazines. Those guys owned their routes. It shocked me that anybody could pony up the average hundred grand it took to get one. More so was that they cleared upwards of twelve G's a month. The idea of getting one of those fat deals myself was more improbable than impossible. Unless I had a rich uncle that I was unaware of, there wasn't a bank on earth willing to front money like that to an ex-con. I tried not to let it bother me, to be content in what I had, but wondered what life could have been if I hadn't taken a pipe wrench to my stepfather's skull. A futile game I played to pass the time.

I was able to smoke a joint before the delivery truck arrived. Mellow and ready for work, I waited my turn.

"Carrier number?" The driver called out as I pulled next to the open swing door.

"Two-fifty-one," I said.

"No shit," he said surprised. "Balentine's got old man Derbie's route. I'll be a son-of-a-bitch!"

I didn't know what to say, so I agreed with him as if anybody ever told me shit.

He handed over a plain manila envelope with my carrier number written in permanent marker. This was the mail. Postcard sized carbon copies written by hand on pink or green paper. A pink slip was an address that requested service stopped or postponed, green was a new start or return to service.

After I loaded my bundles, combined the sections, and stuffed the rolled papers into protective plastic sleeves, I would quickly examine the mail to make the necessary adjustments in my route book. It was a uniquely perfect system used since men did this work from horse-drawn carts.

Webster was considered an affluent area. Living here said you had something more than a good income, that you were a respectable member of society. These were the people who voted with deep concern for who might become president, attended rallies to save whales or ban nuclear power, and leased their vehicles due to tax ramifications. The bulk of my delivery was to modest ranch and barn style homes built sometime in the post-war boom. Nice, but nothing to write home to Mom about.

Then there were the mansions. Ostentatious shrines to wealth that an idiot couldn't deny. I drove deliberately slower in these areas, fantasizing what they looked like inside. I particularly liked the ones that modeled themselves after castles, with towers reminiscent of chess rooks. To heat and cool the gigantic beasts had to cost a fortune. The lawns were big enough to play fifty-yard football games and every driveway disappeared presumably into a hidden garage behind each of the magnum opuses.

In the mail tonight, I had a stop for number seventeen Maid Marion Lane. All the streets where the big houses sat had names taken from the fabled Robin Hood. It was senseless to me, but I guess in the big picture that it made sense. How the fuck could you flaunt Elm Street or Oak Court with any dignity? Sherwood Forrest Avenue and Devonshire Park were names that commanded recognition.

I made the notation in my book using an erasable red grease pencil. The pink slip said to withhold service until July the seventh. Christ, I thought to myself, what kind of wheelbarrow of money did you have to have for a month long vacation? I took one long look at the place. It was a bit larger than the others on the block and probably one of the older ones judging by its slate roof and stained glass windows. Even in the darkness, I could envision the sun's majesty as it filtered through the multi-colored glass.

***

Over the next two weeks, I received a heap more pink slips. It was a mass exodus the closer July came. I hadn't taken off one day since I started with Balentine. My health, despite my regular drinking and cigarette consumption, was outstanding. I didn't have any family who relished the thought of a visit from me or would welcome me if I did show up. The idea of long distance travel made me paranoid and there was no place that interested me enough to overcome my fear.

It fascinated me though how these people lived. Every holiday they left and I couldn't help but wonder where they were going that was better than this? I had found more useful shit in their trash that now furnished my apartment than at the thrift stores. It simply amazed me on Sunday mornings how they threw away couches, chairs, vacuum cleaners, clothes, kitchen tables, televisions, air-conditioners, microwave ovens, washer and dryer sets, stoves, and bicycles like they were obsolete. I had gotten in the habit of grabbing whatever I could after my deliveries. It was practically a second income selling it to the junk shops on Broadway.

One time, a cop pulled up behind me as I was loading a discarded dishwasher. He took my license and ran me through the system. After becoming disappointed I had no warrants, the asshole lectured me for half an hour on the merits of private property. Told me he would be keeping his eye out for me. I still took the dishwasher because I knew how full of shit he was.

One of the few things prison did for me was give me access to any legal book you can imagine. I had earned a paralegal's certificate through a correspondence course and was quaintly referred to as a jailhouse lawyer. None of the guys I ever helped got clemency, but a few got some time reduced on technicalities their pussy court appointed counsels failed to raise. I wanted so badly to tell that Johnny Law to suck it but knew the First Amendment wouldn't protect me from him beating the living shit out of me. The law, however, was clear. Once something was thrown in the trash, possession to it was rescinded. It was why the Feds could dig through your garbage without a warrant.

The Fourth of July was less than a week away when the idea grabbed me. It wasn't like me to become obsessed, especially with anything that could land me back inside a prison laundry room, yet this seemed possible.

The night of the holiday, Webster would be thick with people shooting fireworks and getting loaded. I would have to be on the lookout even at four in the morning for stray partygoers. Cave told me once about an indie carrier who threw a paper smacking some super attorney's drunken wife in the face. That son-of-a-bitch made it his mission in life to ruin the poor guy. He not only lost his route, but he wound up filing bankruptcy because of some mega-jackpot judgment a sympathetic jury slammed down to teach people like him a lesson. "The poor bastard eventually wound up killing himself," Cave told me with unusual sympathy. I guess he must have liked the man.

On the fifth of July, though, the streets would be deserted. The great thing about a community like this was the no bullshit policy enforced with notable encouragement by its residents. By God there was a time and place for such things and when it was over, there would no more open debauchery until Labor Day.

If I was going to do it, that would be the perfect time. The pink slips were clear that the adjoining number fifteen and nineteen Maid Marion Lane had requested delivery be held until the sixth. The idea excited me and made me nauseous all at once.

***

Things couldn't have been more ideal on July the third if I wanted them to be. The delivery was early so I was able to get a head start on the route. By the time I came to Maid Marion Lane it was straight up three in the morning. There wasn't a lit house on the block. I knew the pathetic overnight cop would be catching his predictable nap for at least another hour.

I turned off my headlights after I threw my last paper to number eleven. A cold sweat broke out across my chest. The homes were all pitch black, yet I closely scrutinized each one for the faintest movement. If I caught sight of so much as a stray cat, I would forget the whole stupid thing.

The van motored up seventeen's driveway as if I lived there all my life. A straight shot, it led me to an open area in the rear big enough to house a sailboat and an RV with room to spare. I wanted to turn off the engine, but knew it would draw a hell of a lot more attention to turn it back over than leave it running.

I had brought a flashlight and used it to examine the backdoor. It didn't take a seasoned cat burglar to recognize the ten-digit security pad on the kitchen wall. There was no fucking way I could disarm it.

Even if I could somehow cut the power, it was certain some sort of silent signal would go to the monitoring service. How long would it take some sleepy college student to realize the anomaly and call local police? The little action they saw around here would bring them faster than flies to a fresh pile of shit.

Disheartened, I turned around ready to leave, already chastising myself for such a stupid idea in the first place. That's when I noticed the garage. An exact replica of the house, but not quite large enough for three cars. Oh, what the hell, I thought as went over to it. The side door was windowless and I didn't dare touch the handle. A simple jimmy could set off an alarm. I moved to the garage door that had rectangular traverse style windows at its top. To see inside, I carefully placed a metal lawn chair next to the garage door.

The flashlight shone through the windows thoroughly lighting the interior. There was something underneath a tarp I presumed to be a sports car, six different kinds of exercise equipment, and a model airplane half assembled. The thing that caught my attention was the home office tucked away in the far corner. Three monitors, an enormous hard drive, and a small floor safe in plain sight. It was more than I could have hoped to find. I passed the light to the door, the roof, looking for anything remotely alarm-like. My guess was whoever had set up out here either didn't feel this stuff was worth guarding or simply hadn't gotten around to doing it.

I got back in my van and coasted in reverse backwards to the street. It had taken me twelve minutes to complete my reconnaissance. I shifted the van back into drive, but didn't turn my lights back on until I made a left onto Nottingham Estates. It was going to take all the will power I had to stay sober for the next thirty-six hours. I had to be at the top of my game if this was going to work.

***

Most of the holiday excitement had wound down by the time I started my deliveries. Still, I was cautious. In part to Cave's strong warning and in part to my determination not to do anything that could fuck up tomorrow night's plan.

I hadn't felt this edgy since my first week in the joint. My self-imposed abstinence from pot and alcohol was not helping matters. Every hour that vanished was a victory. The secret to doing time of any kind is to focus on time done, not to go. In spite of that knowledge, I could not help myself.

When I threw my last paper, I drove straight to the nearest Walgreen's and bought an over-the-counter bottle of sleeping pills.

I washed six pills down with a glass of warm milk, set my alarm, and wondered when I awoke if I would have the courage to do this thing.

***

The delivery driver was late. I could tell he had a bad hangover. I was careful to make sure he gave me my correct delivery. The last goddam thing I needed tonight was to come up a bundle short and have to call in a reorder with a van full of stolen shit.

"What bug crawled up your ass, buddy?" he accused me as I dubiously recounted the bundles.

"Just doing my job, pal. Balentine doesn't need any excuse to ride my ass anymore than he already does."

The driver laughed and waved me on. Good, I thought. For a moment I was sure he saw through me, knew I was up to something, and would make sure to comment casually to my boss about it. Now, as I hit the road, rolling and bagging today's edition, I began to relax.

***

I went up seventeen's driveway with the same efficiency that I practiced. In a backpack were the tools I anticipated to use. The flashlight naturally, lineman pliers to snip the computer cables, a small pry bar to bypass the door, a pair of jersey work gloves, and a five-pound deadblow hammer. The hammer was the one thing I didn't know why I packed. It seemed as reasonable as anything else did. I would have packed a portable mixer if I thought it might have been helpful.

I got out of the van with my bag, turned on the flashlight, and walked toward the garage's side door. The thought of getting busted entered my mind one last time. I could turn around right now, no harm, no foul. My body however was overriding my brain as I already had the pry bar in my gloved hands, inserting it in the slight gap between the door and its jamb.

With a quick thrust of power the door came open. I waited for the inevitable howl of an alarm. When I estimated at least half a minute had gone by with no lights or sirens, I rushed to the corner desk. The hard drive screeched on the concrete floor as I drug it out. I cut through the cables with little resistance. It was heavier than I expected and I almost fell in the dark taking it to the van. I checked my watch, seven minutes left.

I picked up the middle LCD flat screen monitor, which was bigger than my TV, and took it next. Four minutes left.

I slung my tools over my shoulder, gripped the safe, and fell to the floor. It was small, not much bigger than case of printer paper, but it weighed a ton. It would take a dolly to move it and probably two men to lift it.

Fuck this, I thought picking myself back up. As I stood a muscle in my leg throbbed. I limped to the door and closed it behind me. Maybe somebody would be coming by to water the plants or some such nonsense. First thing a rational person would do seeing a wide open door is call the cops. It wouldn't take them long to figure a time line. The longer it took them to put the pieces together, the least likely I would look suspicious.

***

For the first time since I had moved into this shithole of an apartment complex, I was glad. Six thirty in the morning and not a soul was stirring. It took the bulk of my remaining strength to carry the computer monitor and hard drive to my second story apartment. I thanked God I hadn't been so greedy as to insist on bringing that safe.

In my medicine cabinet I had leftover Vicodin from a dentist visit. I took four in a heaping gulp, using my hand to cup the tap water and swallow the large pills.

I left the computer stuff in my front room without much thought. The pain in my leg was terrible and all I wanted was to lie down. No sooner had my head hit the pillow than I passed out.

***

I woke up around nine that night. My leg was sore, but nowhere intense as it had been.

The computer was exactly where I had set it. I was curious as to its worth, but also as to its contents. There might be some valuable banking information I could sell on the black market along with credit card numbers. Identity theft was all the rage and I hoped that whoever used this computer had been stupid enough to think something like this could never happen to them.

In an Army footlocker that doubled as a coffee table, I had a collection of electronic whatnots from the plentiful Webster trash. In a matter of an hour, I re-supplied all the wires to connect the monitor to the PC, including a mouse and a keyboard missing the letters Q and K.

I was amazed as the screen came to life in brilliant Technicolor hues. Whereas I expected the standard Windows crap, there was nothing of the sort. The program was custom-made, created exclusively for the owner at a great cost.

No password was necessary and the system automatically logged on. Unlike anything I had seen before, there weren't any icons for the Internet or user interfaces such as Word or Excel. There were however dozens thumbnail photos titled Jenny, Susie, Debbie, Tina, Nancy, Carrie, and so on.

I clicked on a file called Angie003. A girl, maybe eleven, was nude with her vagina spread open. Immediately I closed it. I had seen a lot of fucked up shit in my life, but this was by far a ten on the 'weird-shit-o-meter.' I clicked on another called Diana72. A girl, hardly fourteen, had her hands tied behind her back and was being sodomized by a boy no older than her.

"Goddamn," I said out loud to myself.

I clicked the image closed and wondered what the hell I had gotten myself into.

***

Number seventeen Maid Marion Lane came back right on schedule. I had a green slip in my mail to resume delivery the morning of the seventh. A name and phone number were written on the thin paper. I folded it into a neat square and placed it inside my wallet.

When I drove down Maid Marion, seventeen's lights were on. In fact, every light, in every room was burning and damn near made me slow down. I knew what bothered the owner, why he could not rest, despite the pre-dawn darkness.

I threw his paper and moved down the block. It was my goal to seem nonchalant, pre-occupied with my deliveries, and in no way interested by the glowing home. It personally delighted me this sick cocksucker was tormented. I couldn't wait to finish my route and give him a call.

***

The payphone at Seven-Eleven on Watson seemed a safe place to call from. I had to assume his rich ass had a litany of ways to trace incoming phone calls and their origins. No reason to take a chance at this point. Besides, there was no reason to believe a suitable compromise couldn't be reached.

I dialed the number written on the green slip. The phone rang twice before he answered.

"Hello," he said.

"Yeah," I said, "I'm looking for Roland McKnight."

"This is he," he said, "and to whom am I speaking?"

"Too soon for that sort of thing, Roland."

"Who the hell is this? I should call the police."

"Please, do that. In fact I'll meet you at headquarters with your impressive computer and together we can share the pretty pictures with all the cops. I think that would make everything right as rain, don't you, Roland?"

"I want my property returned," he said. The strong underlying threat had evaporated from his voice.

"Strange as it may sound," I said, "I want something too, Roland."

"You fucking scoundrel," he said.

I recognized his frustration. It was never easy to admit defeat, even more so when your adversary is holding your balls.

"Do you know what they do to sickos like you in the pen, Roland? It isn't pleasant. I can promise you that. You will be raped and beaten on principle alone. Dicks, broomsticks and toilet plungers will be shoved up your ass more than you will be able to count or remember. You'll have your teeth busted out with a weight lifting plate so you can suck cock better. There will be no end to the pain. You will be stabbed, have wire coat hangers shoved in your dickhole, and most likely be castrated by the Muslims to atone for your sins."

I paused to see if he understood. When he didn't seem to have the capacity to reply, I decided to give him the singular option he had outside of serving fifty to life.

"I want something and you are going to give it to me. It won't be extraordinarily difficult for a man such as you, but it won't be painless either. How's it going to be, Roland? You ready to quit fucking around or what?"

"Whatever you want," he said consigned to his loss already, "it's yours. Name your price."

"I knew you would understand."

***

I liked my new van. It had heated seats, a six CD/MP3 compatible HD stereo with Infinity speakers, drop down DVD player, and a monster V-12 diesel engine. It was the van of my dreams.

Cave was certainly impressed by my newfound wealth. It wasn't everyday some rich schmuck thought so highly of somebody like us to do all this.

Even Balentine couldn't understand it. Out of the blue, this guy comes into his office and offers him more than double the market value for the Webster route. If he wanted to shit his money down the drain, he was more than happy to assist the rich jerk.

Cave and I were smoking cigars and drinking coffee. A modest celebration to toast my first night as an indie carrier.

"You have got to be the luckiest fucking guy I have ever known," he said.

"Yeah," I said enjoying the robust flavor of my Churchill, "after all the shit I've been through, I guess I was finally due some good luck."

3 Pigs and A Dog

John sat on the couch with a half-empty whiskey tumbler and stared at the blank television screen. The electric had been shut off three days ago. The gas and water companies threatened to do likewise soon. It didn't matter; nothing mattered anymore.

Nancy had left him taking their two sons. They had moved back east to live with her parents. He wanted to call them but lacked the courage.

He and Nancy had spent thirteen of their fifteen years inside this home. The boys' room still waited ready for their return with beds, toys, and a television. The constant loneliness was an insanity for which he had been unprepared.

As he studied his reflection in the TV set, he could pinpoint the exact moment it all began.

***

Marva, the long-seated watchdog of a church secretary, was dying. Despite a church-wide prayer vigil, a miracle did not appear evident. A diagnosis of cirrhosis, in combination with her emphysemic dependence on portable oxygen, made whatever time she had left precious.

In an emergency meeting of deacons and church elders, it was decided her forced retirement would be necessary. John secretly gave her a hundred dollars in Bingo scratch-offs to assuage his own personal guilt in the matter before leaving on vacation with his family.

***

Debbie was a vivacious mother of four genetically perfect girls and a regular Sunday attendee. Her devoted husband David, a local cop, was either constantly at work or at the church. He tithed their family income regularly but still felt money alone an unpleasant offering.

In the summer he mowed the church's two acres of grass, organized the annual carnival, and gathered volunteers for any number of community improvement projects. In the winter he attached a snowplow blade to his heavy-duty truck and cleared the church lot prior to every service.

Sundays, he drove a church van, chauffeuring the disabled and unable alike to morning services and home again. The guilt he sometimes felt for not being able to do more was a secret he shared with no one.

For all this, he refused compensation, content that what he did was his duty, as if an obedient child to a convalescent parent. How could somebody charge his mother or father for such things? The thought to him was ridiculous.

The church office vacancy was discussed in the brief time Debbie and David shared that evening between giving baths, doing homework and prior to the half-hour family devotional. They decided together that it would be an excellent idea if she applied for the job. The extra money would be helpful now that all the girls attended the church's parochial school.

***

John returned two weeks later and parked in his reserved space. He was an accountant by trade. Often, he thought, he could have been a better used-car salesman. The church accountant for the last decade, it was his father's dream come true before he died.

In the name of the church John had made some wise investments. He had foreseen the Internet bubble about to burst and avoided the catastrophe. In turn the church operated in a surplus of black ink never known before. He, also, had collected on the profits.

Through a series of shrewd, but wholly legal tax loopholes, he would have the money to pay for his children's college education, with more than enough left over to retire early. The interest from well-hidden accounts in the Cayman Islands provided luxuries his current salary could never afford. His recent lavish vacation the most recent of allowances.

John stepped through divided glass doors and walked along the main corridor. The same path that led worshippers to the sanctuary every Sunday led him to work. Prior to the holy room, John made a sharp right turn through a nondescript door with the faded gold stencil *OFFICE*. Immediately he stood in a perfectly square area where general calls were received and visitors waited to be invited into individual offices. Dubbed the bullpen, he was pleased to see it empty.

The secretary's desk was vacant as John gathered his mail. Mostly junk Marva would have had the good sense to remove. He would have to teach her replacement to do the same. An exercise in futility, he thought, teaching a temp to do anything more than answer phones. It would take months to find a suitable full-time replacement but for an even lower salary.

At the desk a flush of water could be heard from the communal toilet down the hall. It had been one of Marva's many chores to keep it clean. He added it to the mental checklist he was already compiling. He enjoyed the thought of such menial duties being passed to some doe-eyed college dropout, watching as her high expectations collapsed. By the end of the week she would use that bathroom to cry.

When he saw Debbie for the first time, radiant in her pink cashmere sweater, at-the-knee-skintight skirt, nude stockings, and bold Italian heels, it was something he would remember forever.

She smiled, still drying her manicured fingertips with an abrasive brown towel, genuinely pleased to see him.

"Welcome back, John," she said. Before he could refuse her, she surprised him with an enthusiastic hug.

He couldn't recall saying, "Thank you," or any litany of pleasantries he stockpiled for such occasions but was certain he had. The rich scent of her perfume tangled in her hair, an aroma of vanilla and wildflowers that made him feel high. So different and brisk than the smell of stale body odor and coffee breath Nancy bid him goodbye with each morning.

Before he realized it, she had left him to answer the phone. "Administration," she answered. "How may I serve you?"

***

In the midst of incoming calls, returning phone messages and e-mails, John made every excuse to call for Debbie. Dutifully she came, glad to fetch him coffee, a file, or something he would normally have done for himself. It was his obsession to find anything she could do for him. He breathed in her fragrance every time she came near until he could taste it, lustfully watching the shape of her ass as she walked away.

Pastor Maury interrupted his morning bliss. He insisted there were many fiscal concerns that needed immediate attention. After the deacon's lunch, they would rendezvous back at his office for a meeting sure to kill the remainder of the day.

He had forgotten about the lunch and knew about all the petty nickel and dime expenditures the pastor would want to review. It was the same thing every Monday. Senseless ramblings by a man concerned with CNN reports over falling interest rates, unrest in the futures markets, and the decline of the GNP when he couldn't even conceive how real money was made.

Despite himself, he enjoyed these sessions, as the pastor listened to his every word. It didn't matter what he told him as long as, in the end, it reassured him that the church's bottom line was blessed.

Today, however, he would not be so indulgent.

"I'm concerned," said Pastor Maury, "in regards to the church's heavy investment in steel. I saw a disturbing piece recently that foreign competition was intentionally flooding the market with product a fraction of its true cost in order to crash the price. What do you think?"

Pastor Maury reminded John of George Orwell's Napoleon. The pig that had assumed the dead farmer's home, wore his clothes, dependent on an ancient entitlement. He knew he was one of the pigs too. The one caught red-cloven, as it were, as he repainted the rules. The difference was his specialty was numbers, not words.

"Pastor," he said, "our position in steel is solid. The rumors of destabilization by foreign interests are simply that, pure speculation. Wealthy brokerages caught outside the boom are trying to drive the price low, buying out the fools. Inevitably they'll create new shortages to send the price higher than before, then liquidate all their holdings at an apex value, probably to do it all over again in oil. Trust me, I have my eye on it."

John's answer, though full of complimentary buzzwords to satisfy the pastor, was too concise. These sessions were designed to obliterate time, validating the high salary he commanded to be the flock's direct spiritual intercessor.

John could sense the pastor's neediness and cut him off by changing the subject. "The office is different with Marva gone."

The pastor nodded and pretended to agree, almost caring. He was concerned with an economy going to hell in a handbasket. Marva was pleasant and whatnot, but he did not miss her.

"How long had she been here?" John asked

"Forty-one years," Pastor Maury said. He knew this information because none of the members would be quiet about it once her retirement was announced. It wasn't until he had made a statement from the Wednesday night pulpit, revealing the church would continue to provide full medical benefits along with Marva's meager pension that the congregation accepted the change. Besides, Pastor Maury furtively thought, she couldn't last much longer anyhow. How much could it cost? He would have to ask John if the church's liability in the matter could be absorbed through a tax shelter.

"That's an amazing duration for any one person, especially a secretary."

"Yes, quite," the Pastor said. "I was wondering about---"

John would not give in. For a change they would talk about what was on his mind. "How long will Debbie be with us?"

"Beg your pardon?" Pastor Maury asked.

"I don't mean to complain, but how soon will it be before the board hires someone permanently? With her family and David's commitments to both work and the church, she is certainly needed at home and, quite frankly, we can't afford to be without a competent secretary to keep a sense of normalcy around the office."

"I sent you an e-mail," the pastor said, "but of course, I should have formally told you the good news."

John thought back to the abundance of spam and nuisance correspondence in his Yahoo account he had deleted. Six hundred messages whittled down to a respectable seventy-five, but he had checked ignore in regard to any church bulletins.

"Debbie *is* the new secretary. Marva formally recommended her to the board by letter and, in your absence, we unanimously agreed." Worried, Pastor Maury asked, "Is there a problem?"

John's sour mood was instantly resolved. "No," he said. "I feel stupid for bringing it up."

Over the next two hours, John randomly made up answers to the pastor's random questions, happy to play court jester to the fool king. It was the least he could do after he had given him so much.

***

Debbie was a wonderful secretary. Before she had dedicated herself to bearing David's children, she had graduated second in her class from Patricia Stevens College. Nothing had been lost in the interim.

The office, barely functional under Marva's wheezing guidance, was now a well-oiled machine. Debbie had purged the bloated cabinets and re-organized the files. Due to her intimate knowledge of church policy she could screen phone calls from solicitors and parishioners alike. The flood of nonsensical crap the office had grown accustomed to was no longer an issue. She came in early and could usually stay late. Debbie was a dream come true.

John couldn't wait to leave home in the morning to see her, to intentionally engage her in long-winded, phony conversations. He delighted overtly in every word. Respectfully she waited on him as he lasciviously undressed her in his mind. John perversely imagined her obeying his every whim in nothing but her high heels and thigh-high stockings. It was far better than his evenings at home with Nancy. His plain, stay-at-home wife found him boring, his work even more boring, and sex a rudimentary chore to be performed. He envied David. If Debbie was as good in bed as she was in this office, no wonder the guy hadn't a complaint in the world.

On the day of her six-month review, Pastor Maury had been invited to speak at the annual non-denominational convention of ministers. The evaluation he would have normally doled out with all the passion of a DMV clerk fell to John.

John called Debbie into his office and asked her to close the door. She sat down across from him with her steno pad in her lap prepared to take dictation. The sound as she crossed her legs of her nylons rubbing between her thighs gave him a powerful erection. Never in his life had he been so glad to have a desk covering his lap.

"Debbie," John said, "I normally wouldn't do this, but in the absence of the pastor certain things need to be addressed." Pastor Maury had given him a handwritten set of notes to go over with her. His chief complaint was that of her attire.

He was concerned because some of the elders had complained that she should choose clothing more demure. Also, that she should quit wearing her hair long and loose, that it should be bound neatly, such as a the tight fitting bun that was Marva's hairstyle. The absurd list concluded with a ridiculous caveat that Debbie should wait to make personal calls until her breaks or lunch hour. In parenthesis he had added (ask if she has a cell phone).

This came from the man who's car was leased by the church, his home mortgage was paid by the church, who used a church credit card to buy tailor made clothes and who had three different country club memberships all paid for by the church. What a prick, John thought.

There wasn't a single positive comment on the Pastor's list. John tore the note into little pieces and tossed them into the trashcan behind his chair. Without a prepared statement, he could feel his pulse begin to accelerate. He wanted to tell her what a wonderful job he thought she was doing, how the pastor could go soak his head if he thought any different, but was afraid he would blurt out something imprudent about her hair or her clothes or her wonderful tits.

"John," Debbie asked, "are you all right?"

"Huh?" he answered. John was so consumed by the moment he didn't quite register what she was talking about.

"You're sweating," she said. Debbie set her pen and pad down hastily and snatched a handful of tissues kept on John's desk. One after another, with the flair a magician would pull colorful scarves from his sleeve Debbie gathered tissues. John never imagined there were so many.

Positioned behind him, she nestled him atop her breasts as she mopped his brow. He felt wonderfully helpless.

Debbie asked, "Are you okay?"

"Yes," he said.

"You might have the flu. Maybe you should go home and rest."

At the mention of home, he sat up, and pulled away from her body. The mere thought brought an immediate vision of Nancy to mind.

"No, I don't think it's that serious," he said.

She hadn't moved, still holding the damp tissues, her midsection next to his ear. It was madness for him having her so close, to treat him with such intimacy. He had heard stories of how junkies got hooked the first time they experimented with drugs. This was how he felt. Addicted to this enchanting, tender creature without the means to satisfy his ravenous appetite.

Unsure of herself, Debbie deposited the used tissues into the wastebasket, among the bits and pieces of the pastor's note, and returned to her seat. The deep consideration for her boss hadn't left her face. John could have asked anything of her from rubbing his shoulders to sitting in his lap stroking his hair and she would have done it. It was her nature.

"Debbie," he said pointing to the blank six-month review except for her name and the date, "this will have to wait. I'm too hungry to focus."

She nodded, collected her few items, and went to the door. As she put her hand on the knob to leave, John asked, "Can I buy you lunch?"

A rush of fresh air infiltrated the closed quarters as she opened the door. No wonder he had been sweating. Debbie flipped her hair over her shoulder and out of her eyes. The smile on her face never faded as she answered. "That would be wonderful. I'll get my purse."

John watched her walk to gather her things and began sweating worse than before. He grabbed a thick wad of tissues from the thin cardboard box to dab away the fresh perspiration across his brow. He felt nervous, as if he were about to vomit. Maybe he really was sick? He stood but had to steady himself against his desk as he put on his suit coat. His asking her out to lunch was spontaneous, accidental even, yet entirely irrevocable.

Debbie fluffed her hair over her collar and shouldered her purse before she walked over to John. The hook of her arm inside his felt natural. His sweat had ceased and the ill feeling instantly passed. He was lighter than air and could barely remember all the reasons he shouldn't be doing this as he escorted her to his Escalade.

***

He had chosen an Irish pub in Westport Plaza recommended by *The Riverfront Times*. John remembered three distinct things from that article: it was located forty minutes away from work, the food was considered authentic, and the atmosphere was private.

They sat in a crescent booth, cozy next to one another. John had ordered a Guinness, explaining away the refreshment to Debbie as 'when in Rome.' In the spirit of friendship, she said she should have one herself. After one taste, she gagged on the dark beer's heavy malt and bitter taste. Embarrassed she explained that she usually never drank much more than a flute of Champagne at New Year's Eve. Unconcerned, John ordered her a Long Island Iced Tea and kept her beer for himself. She found this drink much more to her liking. By the time the food arrived, both drinks were history.

The large servings of wedge cut fries, Ruben sandwiches piled high with corned beef and sauerkraut were effective in distilling the effects from alcohol. The salty food was best chased with ice water to cleanse their pallets.

They ate without much comment or small talk. John barely tasted his food as he watched the humped flesh of Debbie's breast through an opening in her yellow blouse. It was the kind of thing a high-school boy would find exhilarating, and though he did feel some regret, hopeful to see a hint of areola, he did not stop.

He wasn't half done with his meal by the time Debbie mopped the juices and catsup skid marks from her plate. John watched her suckle her bare finger, moaning with pleasure. He thought he might faint.

"John," Debbie said admonishing him.

A cold wave doused his every lecherous thought. How could he begin to apologize? He wasn't sorry for what he was thinking, only for getting caught. He tried to formulate and excuse, but the master of bullshit found himself speechless.

"You've made a mess."

Debbie dabbed a linen napkin in her water glass and began to wipe sandwich dressing from his tie. She leaned her head beneath his chin without a thought. Her amazing scent rushed his senses. The desire to push her head down into his lap, to engulf him wholly into her mouth as she had her finger made him shudder.

John pulled away abruptly as Debbie still held his tie.

"I'm afraid it's ruined," she said annoyed.

Urgent to use the restroom, he excused himself, and scooted out from the booth.

He splashed the cold tap water on his face and stared at his flush reflection. His cheeks were crimson red. The idea of locking himself away in the handicapped stall to masturbate occurred to him.

John shook the notion off, un-knotted his tie, and inspected the stain for himself. The tie was a gift from Nancy. He never liked it and threw it away with pleasure. He unbuttoned his collar, then the button below it. He liked what he saw. Without that restrictive yoke, a small tuft of gray and black chest hair poked out from beneath his white undershirt. He had other ties, a drawer full back at the office he could easily replace it with. He would be surprised if Nancy noticed when he came home.

Debbie waited at the table for John to return. He had planned not to even sit with her again. He would explain they needed to get back to the office. That he had to prepare some suddenly remembered urgent report and he would never, ever do this again.

Before he could say a word, he noticed Debbie had ordered a thick slice of chocolate cake with two forks.

She giggled as he sat next to her again. Debbie spread open his collar for him so that the lapels rested outside of his jacket. "I don't think I've ever seen you without a tie," she said. "You look ten years younger."

She handed him a fork and together they shared the indulgent dessert. The sweet taste melted in their mouths, hardly necessary to chew before swallowing.

John ordered two more drinks while asking the waitress for the check. This lunch could not have been more satisfying than if he had found a million dollars in cash. He signed the receipt and generously added a forty-percent tip, more out of appreciation for the company than the service.

***

They arrived back at the office to the phones multiple lines ringing. Before taking off their coats, Debbie hugged John. Her head to his chest, her silky hair brushing against his exposed neck, she squeezed hard and flat against his body.

"Thank you, John," Debbie said without letting go. "I had forgotten what having a meal that didn't come with a toy was like."

John tried to memorize the moment, to cauterize the feeling into his brain, then contrite, pushed her away. Her eyes were still droopy from the drinks.

"Maybe we can do it again," he said.

"Soon, I hope," Debbie said.

On her tiptoes, she grazed his cheek with a peck. Embarrassed by her own unexpected impetuousness, she spun away, trying to both answer the phone and take her coat off.

John walked slowly to his office and closed the door behind him. In his leather office chair, he was numb. Opening a locked desk drawer, supposedly for confidential church files, he removed a tie similar to the one he had thrown away. Another Nancy had given him that he cinched around his throat tightly as a noose. He pulled out a secret bottle of Bushmills he kept in the same drawer and took a long swallow before locking it inside.

***

The mail came through a slot in the front door and fell with a thump on to the floor. John jokingly thanked God that receiving the mail was still free. He bent over to retrieve the delivery and immediately his head felt like a snow globe held upside down. He brought himself back upright in a delicate, slow process that allowed the chemicals in his brain to gently resettle themselves.

It was eleven a.m. and he had already consumed a full liter of some bottom shelf Scotch called Dragon's Eye. It's fancy label decoration, reminiscent of a serviceman's tattoo, sat boldly among the other generic vodka, gin, and tequila bottles. The label promised the product to be ninety proof alcohol. He bought a case.

A general mess of advertisements for pizza and carpet cleaning hid the single piece of real mail. A letter addressed specifically to him with the prefix of Mr. attached to his full legal name with no return address. If it was another letter from a parishioner forgiving him, he was liable to wipe his ass with it before mailing it back.

Carelessly dropping the mass mailings to the floor, he ripped open the envelope's glued seam. A neat one-page letter was enclosed. The paper was a far better grade than the twenty-pound standard used in offices across America. It was an intentional thing. A subversive physiological mind game played by people who were professionals at the art of intimidation. Through blurred vision, he read:

Dear Mr. Tygett,

This letter is to inform you of recent incongruities discovered in regards to securities purchased by you as head of accounts receivable for our client 'First St. Louis Church.'

Upon examination of internal bank records, it has become obvious you had immediate access to all FSLC's holdings and did engage in unauthorized using of said funds for your own profit.

As you may or may not be aware, this is a direct violation as set forth by the rules of the Federal Trade Commission. As prescribed under the Federal Fiduciary And Trust Act of 1971, you can be held liable for all profits or losses made in commission to the said crime of felonious embezzlement.

You are hereby given notice: if said funds in the amount of $285,327.82 are not returned within the next thirty days by cashiers check to our offices, criminal charges will be filed against you in the Superior Court of Missouri and a warrant for your arrest will be issued.

Sincerely,

M.L. Cooper, Esq.

John re-folded the letter to its original tri-fold shape and placed it in his robe pocket. The idea of possibly going to prison for the next twenty years was almost amusing.

***

The next day he walked into the office eager to see Debbie. Yesterday's lunch was probably the most fun he had had with a woman in years. He felt alive when he was with her and wondered if she made everyone feel like this or was this something special between them? Either way was fine by him.

Betty Sue, a greasy haired woman of simple intellect and enormous weight sat in Debbie's chair. Hands folded together, her eyes like raisins pushed too far back into her skull, stared straight ahead. Jesus Christ, John silently cursed himself as he tried not to grimace at the sight of her.

He removed the rubber band from around the office mail. "Where's Debbie?" he asked.

"Don't know."

"Any messages?"

"No messages."

Her succinct answers, however direct, pissed him off. He left her unmoving heap without any further attempt toward conversation. Except for her short breaths, she was a stone not to be moved.

John lightly rapped on the half-open door to Pastor Maury's office. "Got your mail, Bill," John said.

Busy writing his sermon, with of all things a fountain pen, Pastor Maury normally stopped for nothing except the sound of his own voice. The pastor held his pen hand up and motioned for John to come in, his fingertips stained black with ink. John hoped he wouldn't try to shake his hand.

"Listen to this," he said. John knew better than to think he might have a choice in the matter. "Will you steal, murder, commit adultery, and perjury, then come stand before me in my house? I have been watching declares the Lord! My anger and wrath shall be poured upon place, on man and beast alike, a fire that will burn everlasting and not be quenched. The traitor betrays, the thief steals, but for the liar, the deceiver of my children I shall shew no mercy sayeth the Lord."

The words frightened John. As cliché as it sounded, he felt like the pastor was speaking directly to him. Was this why Debbie had so suddenly and mysteriously gone? John could only confess his purest thoughts in regard to the pastor's excerpt.

"It certainly cuts deep."

"Yes it does, doesn't it," Pastor Maury said admiringly to himself. "This church is due a revival, a re-declaration of the faith. Are you aware tithes are down by thirty percent? Abominable! Did you know that during the Great Depression tithes never wavered by more than seven percent?"

"No," John answered honestly surprised. How did you calculate such things as eggs and livestock given to the church in ways comparable with today's economy? They were a business, like any other, at war with mass market for the consumer's dollar. Unlike Wal-Mart or Sears, people left magnanimous gifts to them in perpetuity. The church had hundreds of thousands worth in premium Blue Chip stocks. It was simply a matter of time before they could be collected. Even the most devout parishioner did not live forever.

"It's not finished of course, but just you wait until Sunday, brother."

"Looking forward to it, Pastor," John lied.

The pastor consumed with his work bowed his head back to the page, deep in thought.

***

In his office, John swished his computer's mouse in tight, concentric circles. He had closed his door, as he presumed the pastor had, as not to have to stare out onto the sight that was Betty Sue.

The monitor flashed to life asking for his password. Entering JOHN316, an enigmatic play upon the famous scripture, it was merely his name plus his birthday. It still delighted him that he had been so clever.

Immediately opening his e-mail account, he reviewed the unopened items for spam. As he checked off the electronic solicitations for enlarging his penis, sexy cam talk with hot sluts, and the usual pleadings for assistance by the scam artists in Nigeria, one caught his attention.

He opened the message titled 'Lunch…?' from Dmartel@wowmail.com as his right hand trembled with excitement.

John,

I had to rush my mother to the hospital late last night. She had a shooting pain in her side and insisted it was a heart attack. Four hours later, she was diagnosed with severe cramps due to constipation. After getting back home around three this morning, I called in sick.

However, after getting the kids off to school, I feel much better than expected. I would love to re-pay you for such a wonderful time yesterday. The forecast is for sunny skies and there is nothing better in the whole world to me than a picnic lunch at Laumier Sculpture Park. I understand if you're too busy, but thought I might be able to tempt you with my world-famous tuna salad on whole wheat.

I'm going out to run a few errands but will check my messages when I come home. Let me know.

Debbie:)

***

John parked his car on the south lot. He walked through the thick, green grass, passing works of outdoor art without any regard for their creativity. The ground was moist. Spring had come early and the mild temperatures had yet to turn the ground hard.

Debbie had said in her last e-mail she would be waiting for him by the Liberman sculpture. A tremendous, five-story work of welded steel silos crisscrossed and painted a vibrant red. It was considered to be the artist's masterpiece according to an on-line search he had made in between e-mails. Aside from its monumental size, John was not impressed.

Debbie wore blue jeans and a flannel blouse. She had pulled her hair back in a ponytail. It made her appear young as a college student. John suddenly felt overdressed in his suit and removed his tie. It was as casual as he could become without taking off his shoes. He had thought of going home to change his clothes, but that would have meant seeing Nancy. There would have been an inevitable interrogation as to why he needed such things, where was he going, blah, blah, blah. It wasn't worth the hassle.

Debbie bound toward him in an exuberant skipping fashion and captured him by the hand. John was surprised he found it necessary to sprint to keep her pace. He was not completely out of shape, not yet anyway, but it reaffirmed his continuing resolution to start using his treadmill again.

The table looked as if Martha Stewart herself had set it. Covered in a red and white-checkered tablecloth, place settings for two had been set. Real china plates accented by gold plated silverware and crystal goblets had been set side-by-side. It exceeded any expectation he had.

"Wow," John said.

"I know," Debbie said jubilantly. "I've been dying to do something like this."

Released from her hand, John sat down as Debbie proceeded to serve their meal. From a quaint wicker basket she placed fried chicken, potato salad, and a small green salad onto each plate. John busied himself by filling their glasses with an already open bottle of moderately expensive wine.

Finished with serving the food, she sat close to him. Debbie would never admit she had begun to prepare the moderate feast before John had accepted her invitation.

Debbie raised her glass. "To new friends."

They taped the fine glasses together with a ring. The cool wine was sweeter than John expected. It was more like liquid candy than an adult beverage. It took will power not to drain it all in one greedy gulp.

The food was a delight. Debbie's culinary skills were at par with her office talents. The rich and creamy potato salad mixed excellently with the spicy chicken. Not much of a greens enthusiast, he rather enjoyed the taste of the complimentary salad lightly coated in an balsamic vinegar dressing.

With the ingestion of each bite, he habitually complimented the meal as "Wonderful," more times than he could count.

Embarrassed, but delighted, Debbie dismissed his compliments. "It's nothing fancy, I swear."

"I'm surprised David isn't big as house. If my wife could cook like this, they would have to bury me in a piano box."

Debbie wiped her hands and took a large drink of her wine. The glass empty, she liberally filled it again, and immediately drank half. "David isn't home much. More often than not he's too busy with work or church projects for something like this."

"Nancy is a good mother, but a lazy wife."

John couldn't believe what he had said. He loved his wife. The second they knew she was pregnant was one of his happiest memories, overshadowed solely by the second time it happened.

"I'm sorry," he said. "I shouldn't have told you that."

She placed her hand over his. The warmth of her soft flesh shot an electric bolt through his body. Debbie began to sob, burying her face into his shoulder. Automatically, he embraced her. As he did his best to comfort her, John nervously looked about the park for any looky-loos. The ever-watchful flock had taught John to be cautious in all things. Certain they had total privacy, he pulled her closer, petting her back.

He kissed her brow. In a tender whisper he pleaded with her not to cry. Then he kissed her again. Her muffled crying finished, she turned her face up to meet his. They passionately kissed, desperate to taste one another.

Debbie stood abruptly and began to clear the table.

John, feeling like the world's biggest asshole, tried to apologize. "Debbie, I'm sorry. Seriously, as stupid as it might sound, it was an accident."

Not saying a word, not looking toward him she continued with the removal of the last few accouterments.

"Please, Debbie," John said, "say something."

Debbie stared down at him with the wicker basket hung in the crook of her arm. Her face was an emotionless palate impossible to interpret. Her hand held out toward him, she pulled him to his feet.

Silently, he followed her back to her car, his hand never leaving her grasp.

***

John's mind was Swiss cheese as he rummaged through dresser drawers and closet shelves. Holes where memories should have been made it impossible to remember.

He gave up for the moment and stumbled to the kitchen. The best remedy to this problem, as to all his problems these days, was to have a drink. He spilled as much liquor over the granite countertop as he did to fill his glass. Quite certain he would soon blackout, he did his best to think about where he had hidden it before all hope was lost.

In a momentary flash of intelligence, it came to him. The details, murky as they were, gave him enough insight as to his next destination.

He navigated the stairs to the basement on his ass, too inebriated to walk and carry his drink. The firm concrete floor was slightly sobering. He stood slowly up using the stair rail for balance. Before he could regain his equilibrium, the full contents of his stomach erupted until he dry heaved.

His pajama bottoms drenched in vomit, his slippers sloshed with the bile. It was here, somewhere. John walked with the directional challenge of a lost, blind man. He felt no pain, but did stop when he rammed his big toe into the immovable object. A government issued footlocker, a surplus leftover he had bought in college that held his most precious things.

He knelt before it in a flop and studied its large, steel latches. It took all his drunken strength to unfasten each one and practically exhausted him. He opened his eyes to find his hands were at work, busily searching through the remnants of his life. Things such as Beatle and Bob Dylan records, a photo album cataloguing his life from infancy through matrimony, and odd little pieces of brick-a-bract he couldn't recall as to why he would have saved them. Then, deep under all the useless shit of his misspent life, he found it.

A black, hard-shell case the size of a lap-top computer. The slides easily pushed out and the lid flopped open. John had mistakenly opened the box upside down. Its contents fell to the concrete floor in a deafening boom. Once the ringing in his ears subsided, John heard the distinct sound of liquids pouring down the built in floor drain. The washing machine was steadily hemorrhaging water through a perfectly round puncture.

He picked it up and held the gun's barrel to his nose. The smell of fresh gunpowder was unmistakable. It must have discharged when he dropped it. Oh well, he thought, as he drunkenly lifted himself up, following the trail of his wet footprints back to the stairwell. At least he wouldn't have to bother trying to load the damn thing.

***

Pastor Maury, by his own admission, held one vice. He was nosy. When he was twelve, an older cousin had taken him to an R-rated film. He remembered little of the movies multiple shoot outs and car chases. What had stuck with him was the main character's advice to the man who eventually killed him. "Keep your friends close, keep your enemies closer."

For years he made it a habit to know what everybody was doing. His wife didn't know it, but he sometimes he had followed her to the grocery store or the mall. One time, at the library, he had lost sight of her in the stacks. Ready to turn around and give up she stood right behind him. As luck would have it, he was standing in the reference department's theology section. Easily able to defend his trip as a research, he picked a book at random without so much as ever reading the jacket. His wife thought it all a wonderful, coincidental surprise and out of sheer guilt he took her to lunch at the good Chinese buffet.

After that little experience, he decided distance was his best friend. No one thought anything unusual of the pastor at his desk surrounded by piles of documents. That was the early nineties, a Jurassic period in comparison with today's technology. No longer did he have to go line-by-line over voluminous phone records, credit card bills, or occasionally having to dig endlessly through file cabinets. Thankfully, those days had passed with the evolution of spyware.

His eyes diligently scanned a computer screen. The program he used now was the best so far. It automatically compiled reports that recorded what websites were viewed and how often, cell phone activity, documents saved and deleted, and most especially how church funds were allocated. He was particularly pleased with the innovation of GPS.

He had replaced all church cell phones with modern Blackberry models. Able to know the whereabouts of each holder via a GPS signal gave him an omniscient rush so awesome he had to reconcile himself against the idea of it being a sin. He did so by convincing himself he was living up to the standard of 'WWJD.' A good shepherd kept count of his sheep.

He had nothing to worry about, yet his paranoia would not rest. Occasionally, he might catch someone perusing Craigslist too often or making personal on-line purchases. It was easy enough to block the user from those sites. If an employee called in sick, he would monitor their location via a chip in their phone smaller than the head of a pin. He had discovered even his most obedient to falsely claim incapacitation by the flu, yet took their phone with them out of habit, while they played hooky at a distant golf course or amusement park with their family. For this he would deliver a penance upon them of endless work until he believed the exhausted sinner had learned their lesson. Thus far, the system worked. He had not once had to reprimand the same person twice.

It was on a crisp fall morning, remotely logged into the network from the comfort of his home study, he noticed the anomaly. At first, he dismissed it as coincidence, but as a precaution, he compiled a spreadsheet that would allow him to see if a pattern truly existed. To his great disappointment, it did. Concurrent to the puritan doctrine he subscribed, it was rare liars told only one lie.

After hours on his computer reviewing personnel files, cross-referencing sent and received e-mails, and calculating text messages by time and volume, he was personally ashamed. How could he have been so naïve? It had been so obvious. Even if he was acting in the best interest of the church, his sin was no less forgivable.

***

John was back on the couch. The gun and the bottle sat beside each other on the coffee table. When the bottle was empty, he could do it. He knew what the mind conceived, prior to a blackout, the body would follow. It was no more difficult than setting an alarm clock. He couldn't count the number of times since Nancy's left that he awoke to find dishes smashed, holes in walls, or lying in one of the boy's beds without a clue as to how it had happened. He knew if he continually repeated instructions mantra-like to himself, he could do this thing. A hopeful consolation was that it would be painless.

The idea of an express ticket to Hell did occur to him. John thought he deserved nothing less. If it would make everything right again, it would be worth it.

If it didn't, well, at least he tried.

***

In the pastor's office Monday morning, John sat ready and prepared to dole out a litany of economic voodoo. He wanted to diverge funds to a Japanese start-up. The NIKKEI was becoming much stronger. Investor's money was returning from the east at a minimum two-to-one. If they moved fast, John could easily triple the holdings of his offshore accounts.

Eager as he was to speak, Pastor Maury was laconic. It was obvious something was on his mind. He got like this sometimes. An unfavorable yet unsubstantiated rumor in regards to a recession had been on the news all weekend. It was the kind of thing liable to disturb any figurehead with a sizable portfolio.

Unable to contain his enthusiasm any longer, John broke the silence.

"Bill, we have an excellent opportunity. If we get moving---"

"Shut-up, John," Pastor Maury said.

His reproach silenced him as if he had cut his tongue out.

"Certain discrepancies have recently come to my attention. I think it would be best for all parties concerned if you were to tender your immediate resignation."

"Bill," John said trying to find an alternate solution, "I'm certain whatever this is, it can be worked out. I can't possibly imagine why you---"

"Stop it," the pastor commanded him. "No more lies." He removed a stapled report from a manila folder and handed it to John. The photocopied list was a compilation of e-mails, text messages and geographic whereabouts that left no doubt any longer as to the reason for the pastor's dismay.

Some of he and Debbie's most personal messages were laid out cold upon the paper. Yellow highlighter lines, smeared across various passages by Pastor Maury, were direct allegations. Intimate thoughts he had shared with Debbie about work, his wife, the pastor and particularly covert messages in regards to his dalliances with church funds were clearly exposed. Each highlighted quotation was an indictment he could not possibly refute.

"Please, Bill," John pleaded, "can't we leave her out of this?"

"I don't possibly see how that is an option."

"She doesn't deserve to be a part of this. Debbie's a good person, regardless what I'm guilty of doing. This will destroy her reputation, her family. Can't you show her some kind of leniency seeing as all David has done for the church?"

"I wish I could, John," the pastor said without sympathy.

"Unfortunately, when you choose to lay with dogs, you're bound to get fleas. I have already called *Mrs*. Martel informing her services shall no longer be required, and furthermore sent a letter outlining the reasons, as I have to your home, as to why your immediate ex-communication from the church is necessary. An emergency private meeting of deacons has been scheduled for three this afternoon. By then, I suspect this matter shall be closed."

"I never meant for any of this to happen," John said. "Please, I'm begging you, let me stand before the congregation, explain myself, apologize. Throw stones and whip me if you want, but leave her out of this. I'm the one who doesn't deserve mercy, not her."

"Noble as that sounds," said the pastor, "I have made my decision. No matter what you say, there is nothing you can say to me any longer that I am willing to hear. You disgust me."

John tore the eight and a half by eleven-inch sheets into quarter-sized pieces and threw them in the pastor's face.

Unmoved, he sat comfortably, hands resting on top of his rounded stomach, not bothering to remove the few stray pieces.

"You hypocrite! I've made this church millions of dollars. You're a rich man because of my disgusting actions. Now, on account of some irrelevant relationship, which not only didn't effect my work, but in spite of everything, made me ten times more productive, I can kiss your ass?"

"Watch your language. Even in this office, this is still the house of the Lord."

"Fuck you, Bill! You pious, sanctimonious asshole. I should compile my own report for the board, maybe they would find it interesting all that you do in the name of the church."

"My records, unlike yours, are all open and more than ready to be reviewed by any member of this church. I haven't promised anyone I would leave my wife for another man's or hidden church funds in a Cayman bank account. You are a moral deviant. The epitome of a wolf in sheep's clothing. As ashamed as I am to ever have been taken in by your schemes, I know I will find absolution. You, on the other hand, will never know serenity again for what you have done."

His fists balled in anger, John was now angry with himself. He was caught and nothing he said could change that fact.

John stood up and silently walked away from the pastor's desk. His steps felt leaden. His hand on the door's handle, he cast one last sincere thought out. "I'm sorry, Bill."

"I'm sure you are," the pastor said.

Defeated, John left.

***

Repeated banging on the front door awoke John from his semi-comatose state. The thuds were as if somebody were knocking using a jackhammer. He couldn't remember how, but the gun was firmly in the grip of his hand. The empty liquor bottle extruded half out from the broken television screen. He couldn't remember that happening either.

He pushed himself up from the couch, holding the gun out as a counter-balance like a surfer trying to stay upright on an invisible wave. Focused on the deafening knock, he stumbled, falling twice before reaching the door.

He crawled on his hand and knees, using the gun to swat away the weeks of discarded mail on the floor. Able to pull himself up by the doorknob, he saw two shadowy figures through the cloudy, white glass with gold ribbon trim. One of the figures was yelling something, the same thing over-and-over, but damned if John could understand him.

Clumsily he unhitched the chain and dead-bolt lock with his gun hand. The mid-day sun blinded him when he opened the door. To shield his swollen eyes, he held up the gun up to block the sun's rays before another brief, much brighter light struck him.

John stood upright and grimly sober as he saw himself lying in the floor. Mixed among the mail, his robe open, the gun no longer in his hand, there was a hole like the one in the washing machine, dead center in his forehead. A puddle of blood collected out the back of his skull. Brains and hair, presumably his, had exploded in mass and covered the walls in tiny bits of red, black, and gray.

The sensation of gently rising overtook him. Allowed one last look toward the doorway, where the two policemen stood, the man on the porch who spoke excitedly into his walkie-talkie was unfamiliar. The other, with his revolver still held high in shock, he knew well. It was Debbie's husband, David.

As a brilliance like none other overwhelmed and guided him from this existence, John was thankful.

Father's Day

Beneath the draped American flag, my father lay in his casket, rotting. I sat in the front row, in chairs especially reserved for family, next to people who were all strangers. My father, benevolent bastard that he was, left my mom and me when I was seven years old. By the next year, he had disappeared, materializing sporadically via a birthday card. The last time he vicariously showed me any attention was thirty years ago.

***

It was a typical Christmas Eve at my grandmother's house. Forced to observe her matriarchal rules, we opened gifts one at a time, allowing others to reverently observe your joy. When I began to tear open the newspaper-wrapped box, you would have thought I was tearing off my mom's skin. She hissed, "It's from your father," as I held the gift up for everyone to see. No one said a word and, like an assembly line waiting to resume, my grandmother gave the command, "How lovely." The next present was opened in silence, while my mom chain-smoked.

He had given me a radio in the shape of a golden apple. It was monogrammed with the expression: "You're the apple of my eye." I couldn't have disliked it more if it had been my dog's severed head. Not only did it more befit an effeminate girl of six than an almost grown man of eleven, it didn't work. The damn thing couldn't pull in one station. I hid it behind the dark velvet drapes in my grandmother's dining room and hadn't thought about it since until this moment.

***

It had taken half my life to get over the whole 'father issue.' Between time spent in therapy, alcohol and weed indulgences that bordered addiction, and the birth of my sons, something finally clicked. My warped childhood ceased to haunt me. The co-dependence of my mother and my father's deliberate inattention became non-issues. They didn't fail to exist; I simply didn't care anymore. I did resolve, however, not to damn the future by repeating my past.

We rose and followed behind the pallbearers. As they loaded the coffin into the open rear door of the hearse, a hand took mine. A woman with yellow teeth the color of her badly dyed hair, held me close to her. If not for the tears welling up in her eyes, I would have pulled back in revulsion. It was obvious she was somebody with a deep attachment to the man in the box.

"You must be Joey," she said in a whisper.

"Yes," I said. It didn't seem appropriate or necessary to correct her. I hadn't been Joey since I stopped believing in the Easter Bunny.

"Will you ride with me to the cemetery?"

"Sure," I said without hesitation, not thinking twice about how I would get back to my car.

The limousine was plain inside. No built-in wet-bar, satellite TV, or speckled-mirror ceiling. The bench leather seats forced the occupants to stare at each other. It comfortably sat eight, but the woman and I were the only passengers.

"You remind me of him, around the eyes," she said.

"Thanks," I said trying my best not to sound offended.

"The last time I saw you was at your first grade play. You were so cute with all that red hair and those big rosy cheeks. I've often wondered how you were doing. You're father refused to tell me anything after the divorce."

"How did he die?" I asked not willing to reminisce upon things I couldn't remember.

"Heart attack. At home…my home, in his sleep. The doctors said he felt no pain."

She said this as if to comfort me. To lay aside any secret concern I might have felt for his welfare. I couldn't have cared less if he had choked to death on a gasoline-soaked rag.

"Don't take this the wrong way, but I don't know who you are."

"How stupid of me," she said suddenly grabbing both my hands inside of hers. The loose flesh covered mine in a field of liver spots and costume jewelry. "Of course you don't."

I felt her trembling nervousness pulse through her. A wave of empathy for this stranger, who wanted nothing more than my brief companionship, displaced me. Although she was foreign to me, I had a compulsory need to treat her with care.

"I'm sorry. I didn't mean to---"

"Don't apologize, bubula. I'm the one who should apologize," she said. "I'm your aunt, Rachel."

Now I was the one trembling. I knew so little of my father. The bit I did have was a selective oral history extracted from my mom like teeth from a whale. He was Jewish, a veteran of the Navy, he had been married to Mom for eight years and, his last known employer was a defunct carburetor machine shop in north St. Louis. Beyond that, I didn't have a clue.

"It's nice to meet you," I said sincerely.

"Joey," she said with a voice of new found intimacy, "your father did you wrong."

I wanted to say something but could not speak. As I nodded my head slowly in agreement, I hoped she could elaborate.

"You were such a precious boy. So smart, you could read before you went to school. Ah, such a good boy. It broke my heart how he turned his back on you. I tried for years to make him do the right thing, buying birthday cards and presents for him to send. Most of them, unfortunately, didn't make it and after awhile it was a waste of time to try. The drugs, that goddamn cocaine, controlled him like a dog on a leash. For years, bubala, he would go missing. Many was the time I had no idea if he were alive or dead.

Then he would show up, as if nothing was wrong, broke, strung-out, needing shelter and food. Always I took him in. After he was well again, I would always encourage him to see you, that it was never too late. He said he couldn't until he had a good job again, a nice place to live, something to show for his life. Then he would be gone. Back to his life of bars and drugs. It has been my constant sorrow knowing he had a son, a good boy, when I had nothing."

The car came to a slow, gentle stop in the gravel road. Daylight consumed us as the driver opened the door, and we walked towards the open grave. His casket, the flag removed, waited to be lowered into the earth. My newfound aunt Rachel and I sat in cheap, plastic chairs that tilted slightly on the uneven ground

A Rabbi spoke eloquently of the stranger I called my father. The words sounded wonderful but were like a song in another language. After a prayer in Hebrew, we stood to repeat the closing words after him. Those around me recited the words by rote that I couldn't understand. I humbly whispered the Lord's Prayer in substitution.

On the ride back to Aunt Rachel's house, I told her about my life. The years of struggling to make ends meet, first as my mother's son, then as a husband and father. I left out the suicidal rages, the manic depression, and the self-loathing. It was a rare opportunity to present myself anew.

The upper-middle-class condo was luxurious. At least twenty people, some of whom I recognized from the funeral milled about the main floor. Aunt Rachel excused herself to use the powder room and encouraged me to mingle. I was family after all.

Little groups of people had formed like islands. As more came through the door, they quickly found their particular group. I decided my best course of action was to comfort myself on my aunt's expensive whiskey and try to avoid eye contact.

A short, fat man whose size and color reminded me of a tomato was loudly greeting everyone. Despite his volume, he didn't seem to bother anybody. Most smiled and some even laughed as he approached, then moved on to the next person. In sales, we called it 'working the room.' I had to admit he was good. It was only a matter of time before he would reach me.

He shook my hand in an ironclad grip. "Ronald Goldman, attorney at law. Pleased to make your acquaintance."

"Nice to meet you, Ron," I said hoping that was all there was to this.

"I'm fairly familiar with everyone here, but you, sir. Might I inquire at to who you may be?"

"Cut the shit, pal."

"I beg your pardon?"

"The song-and-dance routine. Great icebreaker, but completely unwarranted. I bet you don't know more than five people in this room by name."

"That's quite an allegation, sir."

"It's the truth though, isn't it? You haven't taken your coat off, so I'll assume you're here on business, and won't be staying longer than necessary. None of the women here hugged you, but every man has made it a point to shake your hand, so you're not family. The clincher, though, is that you introduced yourself to me via your occupation."

The smile on his face was looming as when he first walked in, yet the good humor in his voice evaporated.

"You're Joe's son, correct?"

"Correct."

"Pursuant to law, you are his only living relative outside of his sister and the heir to his estate upon his demise."

From inside his coat pocket, he removed an envelope the size of a sheet of paper, folded in half, and sealed by a red wax seal. A large letter 'G' was stamped into the hardened material that matched the oversized middle finger ring on his right hand. The ostentatious display of wealth and minor power was easier to read than the back of a cereal box. He was the kind of self-inflated jerk I dreamed of walking into my office. Nothing but the best would be good enough for his royal ass. Guys like him made my sales goal every year.

The neatly handwritten script was addressed to no one in particular.

Last Will & Testament

of

Joseph Irving Cohen

The name was the same as mine except for the abbreviated junior at the end. It suddenly occurred to me that the name we had shared was now mine alone.

The lawyer handed me his card. "Should your require any further assistance, call me." I didn't even look at it. "I was intimately familiar with your father's affairs and considered him a close, personal friend."

I loosely shook his hand, more out of formality than gratitude. The idea of suddenly having my father's most intimate details thrust upon me was disorientating. Never in my life had an envelope felt so heavy in my hands.

I stepped outside to find some privacy. In a small garden I sat down on an ornamental metal bench hardly larger than a stool and tore open the envelope.

Inside were three stapled, legal-sized pages of standard litigious crap constituting my father's will and a plain, white envelope with the name 'Joey.' I presumed the will was in accordance to every law made and hardly glanced at it. The curious little envelope consumed my attention. I recognized the handwriting the moment I unfolded the letter.

Dear Joey,

If you were hoping for a decent payday out of this, tough luck kid.

There ain't much of nothing left I didn't snort or smoke or some bimbo didn't con out from me. I hope you're doing better.

I'm sorry about not being there. It couldn't have been easy growing up without a dad. I heard you got a couple kids yourself now, so maybe you can do for them what I didn't for you.

No matter what your mom or her family says, it wasn't easy for me. It's not like I woke up one morning and said 'Fuck this, I'm gone.'

When I left I had every intention of seeing you every weekend. Taking you to ball games, carnivals, spoiling the living shit out of you before having to bring you back.

Usually, we hung out eating Chinese food from the place I lived above. You loved the moo goo gai-pan and ordered it every time. When you went home, I would get so depressed, I would drink until I quit missing you.

Then one weekend your mom said you couldn't come. I went nuts without you. Before Monday I "accidentally" took a whole bottle of Valium. That was the beginning of me losing you. After that no judge in his right mind would have allowed me unsupervised visitation.

When I moved, I didn't tell your mom. She was pissed (what's new) and swore I would burn in hell before I would see you again. In a sense, I suppose she kept that promise.

My life without you has been something I wouldn't wish upon my worst enemy. I still carry a picture of you from the fifth grade your grandmother gave to me. Whenever I felt like I couldn't take it anymore, that this time I wouldn't call for help, I would pull out that picture. Your smile never failed to give me hope. It reminded me once I was a good man.

I hope to give you this letter in person one day. Maybe cop a squat at the tavern together, share a beer, and get to know each other. If Ron gave you this letter, that isn't going to happen.

Be good to yourself, son.

Love,

Dad

After I was able to pull myself back together, I folded the letter and put it back in its envelope. The tears I cried were not sad or from a sense of melancholy, but relief.

When I came back into the house, through the sliding glass door, the mourners had tripled. The large room now felt crowded.

I found the buffet and made myself a plate. At the end of the smorgasbord, I noticed a small table of pictures.

They were photographs of my father, a collage of his life. There he was, a young, healthy stud sitting on a motorcycle. In another, he was dressed in black tie and tux. One in particular struck me. He was forever captured pushing me on a playground swing, a smile on his face that matched the glee of mine. Picking up the color snapshot, I put it in my pocket next to his letter.

Before I could pull my hand from its hiding spot, an accusatory voice made me feel as if I was a child caught taking cookies without permission.

"What are you doing?"

"I was, I mean…" I floundered in excuses, then regained control of myself. I had no reason to lie. "He's my father and as sad as it might sound, I don't have one picture."

"I like this one," he said pointing to my father with his arm draped about a stunning brunette.

"Me too," I said not caring, relieved to have the focus off my theft. "She's beautiful."

"She's my mother."

The words he spoke, simple enough to comprehend, stunned me. The picture was obviously an intimate portrait of two people in love.

I turned to face him, to ask him what this was all about, and temporarily lost the power of speech. To look at him was like staring into a mirror, but ten years younger. Except for his shock of thick black hair he wore shoulder length our similarities were astounding.

"They never married. Joe said marriage was a one-time deal. I'm kinda glad they didn't. They mostly fought when he was around. I haven't seen him in years."

"I'm Joe," I said holding out my hand.

"I know who you are. I've known you all my life. That's why I came here today."

He pulled me into a spontaneous embrace, which I did not resist. He was trying not to cry and I held him until his insecurity passed. When we were finally able to separate ourselves, he formally introduced himself.

"I'm Brian, your brother. Illegitimate, but all same. It's good to finally meet you."

We talked non-stop for the next two hours, ignoring everyone else, filling in each other's life with our father's memory. He certainly had more to say, and I cherished every word.

After excusing himself for the restroom, Aunt Rachel sat next to me, rubbing her hand up and down my back as to soothe me.

"I was hoping you two would find each other. I hope you're not mad."

"No, why would I be?"

"It was a secret my brother insisted on keeping. I promised him I would never tell. He always thought you would hate him if you knew."

"That's stupid."

"Men are stupid. The secrets they keep." She stopped, wanting to say more, to elaborate on the idiocy of the opposite sex but refrained. "What will you do now, Joey?"

"Brian and I were talking about going out. Maybe getting to know each other some more."

She patted my knee and stood up. "Come with me."

I walked with her past the guests, holding her hand oblivious as to where we might be going. When we came into the sanitary kitchen of chrome and marble, she released me and asked that I would wait. For a moment, I stood alone, armed with my father's picture and letter. The knowledge of his other life, of my half-brother and aunt, this entire family I did not know, yet belonged to began to disconcert me.

Before I could panic and leave, Aunt Rachel returned. She closed my hand into a fist as she placed a set of keys in my palm.

"In the garage, bubula. It was your father's pride and joy. The one thing, no matter how desperate he got, he wouldn't sell. When he needed peace, he would go to it, never taking it out of my garage."

I kissed her on the cheek and promised I would come back soon to visit.

I found Brian and together we went to the garage. Next to a piano-gloss black Mercedes, sat a cherry red convertible Stingray Corvette with the top already down.

After cleaning the out empty beer cans and liquor bottles, making sure to put them into their proper blue recycling bins, we slid over the doors, down into the custom bucket seats. The super-charged motor roared to life when I turned the key. The rumble transferred through the chassis with and erotic vibration reminiscent of a quarter-fed motel room bed.

"Where should we go?" Brian asked.

"I know a good tavern," I said.

Walking Uphill

The doorbell rang, and I wasn't ready yet. Either Danny was early, or I was extremely stoned. The later was probably closer to the truth. I peeked at him through the blinds and signaled that I needed one more minute. He shrugged his bony shoulders and sat down on the ledge to roll a joint.

I had worked all morning writing a new song. The first few parts had come quick and easy. It had a solid chorus with a sharp hook that I knew would grab people's attention.

The song was about a regretful band of musicians. Guys who had achieved what they had always dreamed of only to find it was all lies. Fame did not mean happiness, money did not equal success, and sex was not love.

Finally getting my shoes on, I joined Danny on the porch. The sun was at our backs, still steadily rising in the east. The torturous heat of the sun was still a couple of hours away, but the humidity already made the air sticky.

The stillness at eleven in the morning was beautiful and rare. An occasional empty school bus or the sounds of distant lawn mowers were all that disturbed the peace.

Danny had recently dyed his hair blacker than a concert T-shirt. It gave him a sickly look that accentuated his pasty white skin, making him look ghoulish. Underneath his black hoodie with a white fanged skull decal on the back, I knew he was wearing a Zeppelin, Sabbath, or Doors shirt underneath. Those bands were immortals to us. We felt obligated to offer our undying tribute to them twenty-four seven.

We sparked up the skinny heater Danny had rolled. Our friendship was based upon three things. First and foremost was the music. There was nothing we did that wasn't in the hope of becoming better, more successful musicians. Second was weed. We smoked it, sold it, and simply couldn't imagine life un-high. The third thing, albeit odd, was the only thing we actually did based in reality. We walked.

Miles upon miles we tested ourselves to see how far we could go out. We always made it back home, although there were times I wondered if I was going to make it.

Once, we must have walked at least fifteen miles. No water, no money, and hotter than hell. By the time we made it home I was seeing black spots. Danny, however, was a rock. While I sat high on Vicadin and weed, drinking gallons of Gatorade the next day, he walked. He had done a five-miler to stay loose. I told him I had ate an entire large Imo's deluxe by myself and we both laughed at the insanity we called our lives.

Taking the nubby remainder, I smoked the last hit and tossed the roach into plastic ashtray to die out. It would be there when we got back, then we could add it to our hard times collection. It was stoner insurance against the future when we would be to broke to score.

Danny and I began to stretch out our calves using the concrete stairs. I used the upper set while he did his on the lower. We never talked about where we might go, we would just start walking. Danny had been doing this far longer than I had and had dozens of different courses laid out his mind. Secret maps he alone knew and shared only when we walked. I trusted him unquestioningly as my guide.

We didn't calculate by distance as much as by time. Three hours was his norm and generally my max. The asphalt streets, the grassy overgrown empty lots, the immaculate graveyards, and the never-ending sidewalks of south St. Louis disappeared under our worn shoes. The idea was to stay in constant motion. Why, I didn't know, but it was a rule I never questioned.

Danny stuffed his hands into the marsupial pouch of his hoodie. "You ready?" he asked.

My calves were stretched and loose, prepared for coming fatigue. I welcomed it, and the endorphin rush by which no drug could compare.

"Yeah," I said. "Let's go."

Within ten minutes we were damn near to Carondelet Park. Danny only walked this fast when something heavy was bothering him. I knew better than to ask what. He would tell me if he wanted me to know.

"George and me are going to the Pageant Thursday. Kidz Without Eyes are playing. Supposed to be a killer show. You coming?" I asked.

"No. I don't think…" Unable to complete the sentence Danny lied. "Band practice."

"Right," I said. "I forgot."

I lied too. In my whole time hanging out with him a show always trumped anything else. Your father's wake, your brother's wedding, your sister's graduation all came second to going to a show.

"So you guys are practicing on Thursdays now?"

"Huh? What the hell are you talking about?"

"You always practice Mondays and Wednesdays."

"Are you my mother now?"

"No man, I was---"

"Mind your own fucking business."

"Sorry, dude."

"Whatever," Danny said. He pointed his black nail-polished finger south by southeast. "Cut across," he ordered.

Obedient as a dog, I followed his command. In a light sprint, despite the lack of traffic on Loughborough, we left the park much earlier than usual. Before we slowed we were at the crest of a long downhill slope that lead to a spillway dubbed River Des Peres.

By the time we came to the bottom, my shins were on fire. Germania Avenue was one of the few stretches in the city absent any sidewalks. Any time of the day, the road was busy. Forced to walk in the uneven, pot holed ledge, the noise and wind of the cars constantly passing by made it impossible to talk.

I didn't mind though, it was a beautiful day. The forced silence gave me the leisure to think to myself without distraction. I seriously considered how much longer I was going to be able to keep playing the rock star. My wife had given birth to our beautiful baby boy almost a year ago. By next weekend, every relative we had would come to fill our one bedroom, one bathroom house to celebrate the fact.

After the cake was cut, and all the cousins were done fighting over the new toys, it would begin. Somebody would ask how work was, and I would say fine trying to appease their morbid curiosity. It was never enough. Then it was "do you like it?" and "any hope of going full time this year?" and "don't forget you have a family to think of now". It wasn't ever "how's the band?" or "write any new songs lately?" or, God forbid, "you're band is so awesome!"

I was thirty now and beginning to doubt my life choices. When I was twenty-something, with no responsibility outside of self-indulgent habits, I had grandiose visions of being in a world famous band. In a new city every night, worshipped by thousands. I dreamed of staying high on primo Amsterdam grass and groupies who wanted nothing more than to make my every deviant fantasy come true. So far, I hadn't even been close.

I had sacrificed countless hours at the altar of rock-n-roll. So much wasted time I could have been in college or building a career. Many of my friends now had nice homes in the county. They drove to soccer practice in lavish mini-vans that were more like rolling homes. Whereas I had held a succession of brainless, labor intensive jobs, they had become responsible adults with careers. At best, I had only grown older in a chosen profession that equivocated success with youth, good looks, and occasionally talent.

The grass causeway finally gave way back to the comfort of the sidewalks. We walked side-by-side with me always next to the street. Danny had, in my opinion, an irrational phobia of a car leaping the curb and crushing him to death. The idea of dying didn't really bother me as much as living did. Besides, if it did, we were both dead meat anyway.

We ditched the street and headed down one of the nameless alleys we knew were safe. While Danny took a pee behind a dumpster, I rolled a generous finger-thick joint. After we smoked half, we resumed the walk.

Danny and I stuck to the interchange of alleys for awhile. I wasn't sure of where it was all leading, but I was contentedly stoned. Happy enough to feel the sun on my face and the ground melt away under my shoes. The song I had been working on so diligently before Danny came over played in a continuous loop in my mind. I was close to finding the elusive chords to the bridge when Danny interrupted my thoughts.

"Little Lisa is pregnant," he said.

"So what," I said. Danny had been especially quiet so far. It figured now, when I was starting to find a groove, he wanted to gossip. "She's a slut anyway. Half the bands in St. Louis have screwed her. It was only a matter of time before some poor schmuck drew the shortest straw."

"That's cold blooded man. She's a human being."

"She's a cum dumpster. I feel sorry for the baby she's gonna have, and more sorry for the dumbass who didn't have brains enough to wear a rubber with her."

We cut left out of the alley and found the sidewalk again. Great oaks shaded the street and the immediate climate change was refreshing. The alleys were the quickest route to anywhere by foot but offered little in the way of scenery. I loved to walk here passing the evergreen lawns of the perfect homes. I imagined that someday all my hard work would lead me here. In the basement I would have a recording studio with every electrical device imaginable. My kid would go to a private school and my wife would have friends who drank wine to the pass the time. A pipe dream that connected to all the other broke plumbing that was my life.

"You're wrong about her," Danny said.

It took me a moment to register he had even spoken, much less what he had said. I was becoming frustrated with his one-track mind on the subject. We had some of the best conversations on these walks. Philosophy, art, music, television, movies, religion, and countless others to forget the pain in our legs or the subconscious desire to sit down.

"So what if I am," I said. "So what and who cares? You're acting like it's your problem."

"It is. Sort of."

"What the hell does that mean?"

The street dumped out abruptly to a main artery. We stood on the corner and waited for a break in the noonday traffic. The smell of McDonald's French fries mingled among the car exhaust and made me ravenous. When I got home, I was going to nuke a bowl of nachos el hoosier dumping salsa over Doritos topped with sliced American cheese. I would eat until my stomach ached in bloated tension and forced me to sleep until Cheryl came home. She wouldn't care as long as there was a fresh bowl packed in her pipe and she could unwind a little before the band showed up for practice.

She had been hinting lately that maybe we could start to practice over at George's. It worried her that the volume wasn't good for the baby's ears. He certainly couldn't sleep until we were done. I wasn't mad at her though. Cheryl was never what I would call a bitch or a nag. It was rare she ever had an opinion regarding my musical ambitions at all. This, however, was about the kid and change was inevitable.

The simple pleasure of hearing our footsteps smack in the minor echo of garage doors and chain link fences comforted me. This alley was the road home. No more turns, just a straight and steady grade that, practically put us on my front door step.

"What do you do now?" I asked him.

"Don't know. Can't really do much of anything except wait for the results back from the clinic. She named me and another guy as being possibles. I wasn't going to do it, let them test my DNA, but Little Lisa was out of her mind for it. Said if I didn't, the case worker would have a fit and her benefits would be less and a whole bunch of other shit that made me wish to God I never did it with her."

"Do you think it's you?"

"Knowing my dumb luck, probably."

"Maybe you'll get lucky."

"Yeah, maybe."

We walked the last few blocks home and my shirt clung to my skin with perspiration. I licked at the droplets of sweat around my mouth aching for a drink. My hands trembled and I was suddenly cold, the first sure signs of heat exhaustion. To me it was a badge of honor to push myself so hard, to test my limits in a vain effort to raise them higher. I figured what didn't kill me made me stronger. No pain, no gain was my motto. In hindsight, it was just plain stupid.

I found instant comfort when my house came into view. In a moment I would be rinsing off under a cold water shower. After my outer cool down, I would replenish internally with junk food, pot, and cigarettes.

"You gonna' be okay?" I asked him.

"Yeah," he said, "it is what it is."

"I hope you luck out man."

"Me too," he said but we both already knew.

Little Lisa sat on the stairs at Danny's house, crying.

No More Bets

Kenneth and James sat on skinny barstools with chrome legs and sparkling plastic seats. For a Wednesday morning, the Hard Times lounge was quiet. Except for the bartender and the sleeper in the men's room, the place was theirs.

It had been an unusually successful morning. James had struck gold at the bottom of Highway Forty. Holding a piece of stained cardboard, especially careful to write 'God Bless You' at the bottom in letters bigger than the rest, a Hummer had stopped. The driver handed him a fifty.

Kenneth saw James hoofing it, honked, and offered him a ride. He had dropped his mother off at work and had time to kill. Mutually they decided James' good fortune would be best spent on whiskey. The gross amount afforded them the luxury to drink as gentlemen, not as bums from paper-bags.

"It's an easy score, man," Kenneth said, knocking back his second shot of bourbon.

"No such thing," James said.

They had bought a pitcher of draft beer. Generously filling their mugs, careless about foam or spilling, they upheld the bars' theme: *The Hard Times Lounge. Where good times begin.*

"We go in on a Saturday. Ain't nobody there. Shit, ain't so much as a camera to watch us," Kenneth said

"No cameras," James agreed, "but what about guards?"

"Like I said, man, it's Saturday. Building is shut down."

"Then how the fuck do you plan on getting in?" Refreshing his beer, he wished Kenneth would shut-up about it. "The police are lazy, but they ain't stupid. I would think two fuck-ups carrying computers through a broken glass window might even get those fat bastards to stop."

"We ain't gonna' need to break nothing."

"I suppose you have a key?"

"No, but I've been watching this place. I've got it worked out. What I need now is a stand-up guy to do this shit with."

James held up two fingers. The bartender automatically filled two shot glasses with the bottom shelf bourbon. James peeled off a five, handing it over, refusing the fifty-cent change back. The bartender acknowledged the meager tip with a nod, before he returned his attention to the sports page. The Rams were a joke this year, breaking his heart, and emptying his wallet.

"I don't know. I've heard a lot of these 'easy money' ideas in my life. So far, every guy winds up in the hole."

"That's 'cause they were stupid. Too fast and too greedy for their own good. Like I said, I've got it worked out."

"What the hell does that mean?" James asked. He regretted his curiosity as he wiped the foam from his mustache.

"Inside that building, all the way in the back is the film library. You come in, sign a log, and go back passing by all these fancy offices."

"You want to rip off the library?"

"No. I want to steal the office next to it blind."

"Sounds iffy to me."

"I've already done a practice job."

James choked slightly in mid-swallow. In their business of living hand-to-mouth, there was no practice. Trial and error was their teacher.

Kenneth sat straight, grinning smugly at having stumped his pal.

"You have got to be shitting me," James said. Holding up two fingers again, he peeled off another five.

"I got the idea about six months ago," Kenneth whispered as if someone might overhear. "I was standing in the film library, checking out the cartoon DVDs. Except for the jerk behind the counter unpacking delivery, ain't nobody else around. I heard somebody say something and at first I thought it was the library guy, but shit he's busier than a man at the gates of hell selling bibles, so I know it wasn't him. Then I heard some laughter and some more talking. It was coming through the wall. Tapping a little here, a little there, the wall separating the film library and the business next door can't be more than foot thick. Wouldn't take nothing more than a recip saw to tear open a hole a truck could drive through."

"Why not use the door?"

"It's got a motion sensor attached. Saw it when I pretended to get lost looking for the library."

"Ain't the library got one too?"

"They got shit. A push bar with a built in alarm. Goddamn thing ain't connected to nothing 'cept a nine-volt battery."

"No shit?"

"No shit. So that got me thinking," Kenneth said, "how do I get inside. I tried the front door. Used a crow bar on that son of a bitch for an hour. It was useless. Damn door is sealed by a magnetic lock. Couldn't go in that way without making a real mess. Then I tried a side door where everybody is forced to go smoke, same deal. Now at this point, I'm thinking fuck it, I'm going home when I see two garage doors. I'm standing there with my jimmy tool in my hand at two in the morning when the exit door starts to go up. Shit, man, I froze up like a statue. I thought my ass was grass."

The bartender ignored James' two-fingered request, as he talked as into the phone behind the bar. It didn't take a lip reader to see he was about to waste another three bills on the Rams.

"Then this little silver number comes whipping out. Never saw me. The garage door still hanging open, I walked in. I opened the first door I came to and, presto baby, I was in the building. I went straight to the film library, ready to haul ass if the alarm went off. When it didn't so much as peep, I could've died."

The bartender set another two shots down and grabbed the five. He reassured himself with all the reasons the team could win this Sunday, at the very least beat the nine-point spread he locked in with his bookie, as he separated his tip from the till.

"The room was mine. I stuffed my coat pockets with movies, then went to leave. When I turned that handle, I couldn't believe it."

"What?" James asked.

"The goddamn door was locked from the inside."

"Holy shit!"

"Tell me about it. I yanked and pulled on that motherfucker, but it was tight. There wasn't a gap big enough for my tool much less a stick of gum. Walking around the room, I started trying the doors. Gotta be a fucking door every six foot and every one locked. The last door had a panic bar with big letters 'EMERGENCY EXIT ONLY' above the handle. Turned out to be another white elephant."

"Unbelievable," James said. The story beat the one channel TV above the bar, and Kenneth's company was far better than drinking alone.

"I walked down the stairwell until I was right back where I started. Walking back to the garage exit, it hadn't occurred to me how the hell I was gonna get out of there. I figured maybe there was a pressure plate or an electric eye that popped the garage door open when I saw it."

A new pitcher of beer replaced the empty. The bartender, primed by James' regular tipping, made sure to give them new frost covered mugs before leaving the bar to wipe off tables.

"A big red button like on that game show with the whammys. All I did was push it, and 'open sesame', the thing went up. I was amazed it was so simple. Finally, I went to my van and got the fuck out of there before somebody got nosy."

James sipped his beer. The buzz from the alcohol mixed well with the story. Definitely, not the first incredible tale told at this shellacked counter, certain not to be the last. First, the windfall from the guilt-laden yuppie, now this. James had read his horoscope this morning before he started his work. The psychic had proclaimed this to be his lucky day. He generally didn't lend any credence to such nonsense. He read it for laughs. This, however, was too good to be true.

"So, what's the plan?" James asked.

***

December twenty-third and the streets were deserted. A front had moved in bringing bitter cold and single-digit temperatures. Kenneth sat on a piece of cardboard near the garage door, drawing no suspicion from the occasional police cruiser. The bored cops didn't see anything but another bum. He was frozen to the bone, yet watched the door with the vigilance of a mother over a sick child. James sat ready in the van, waiting for Kenneth to make his move.

They had made a connection with a fence. He promised seventy per hard drive, twenty-five per monitor, if they were flat-screens, and a willingness to take any miscellaneous items if they were electronic. The way the world was heading, every damn thing worth taking had a computer chip. This haul should be enough to put him on fat street for awhile. He could buy some gifts, even if it would be after Christmas. It would be more than enough to see him through to the spring thaw. After that, he had no solid career plans besides stealing copper from foreclosed homes. It wouldn't pay off anything like this, but opportunities like these were practically one in a million.

Kenneth stood up as if an electric jolt shot through him. He floated backwards into the darkness like a diver going underwater.

James watched, as a crack of light grew larger. A Hummer, a duplicate of the one from the off-ramp, leisurely drove out. The driver, busy with his cigar, CD player, and his cell phone, never saw Kenneth walk into the garage.

The door closed and for a moment James thought about leaving. It wasn't too late. As he put his hand on the door handle, needing to merely decide in which direction he would go, the garage door rose open again.

Kenneth stood, posed with his hands crossed over his chest.

James moved his hand from the door back to the steering wheel, gently put the transmission into drive, and steered the van through the open garage door.

***

They sat in the cab of the parked van, sharing a cigarette. Mainly, Kenneth needed to get warm again. He had been almost ready to give up after three hours crouching on the piss and spit stained concrete.

James wished he had remembered to bring a pint, something to calm his nerves, but glad he hadn't. He needed a stone cold sober mind to do this work. When this was all done, he promised himself a case of top shelf whiskey and week in a hotel. It was akin to the promise given to those raghead assholes, the one that guaranteed seventy virgins in heaven. The difference was his chances living through this experience were far better than Abdul's.

Kenneth took the last drag from the cigarette and rubbed his hands together. "Let's go to work."

James carried a fifty-foot, orange extension cord; a reciprocating saw; a can of red spray paint; and a three-pound sledge. Kenneth, who walked with no urgency, led the way comfortable as a man in his own home, James hoped his friend was right. The last thing he needed was to go back to the joint. A felony B&E was a mandatory five years in Jeff City with guys who had nothing to do all day but beat the fuck out of guys like him.

They used the stairs to get to the first floor ignoring the beautiful, all-glass elevators.

The elevators reminded James of the extravagant hotel in Kansas City where he had honeymooned with his ex-wife. He had almost gotten into a fistfight with the manager over the bill. Seemed an unreasonable cost to him for what amounted to nothing more than a bed and a toilet. Pamela, the ex, got him to pay the bill and apologized to the queer like he had shit in the hotel swimming pool. That should have told him what life was going to be like married to her. Unfortunately for Pamela, it took another five years before she realized he couldn't change. Last he heard she had went out to Vegas to deal Tarot cards.

They passed the men's room and followed the signs to the library. Kenneth pointed to the office door behind where their score laid. The slim glass pane in the door offered no insight, and they moved down to the library's door.

The plain brown handle looked formidable. A lock was built into it presumably to arm its hidden siren that would announce a trespasser with a shrill whistle.

"Here goes nothing," Kenneth said.

If the damn thing sounded, it was James job to smash it to bits with the sledge.

The clack of the door's lock released and, as before, the alarm failed to work. It was nice to see such consistency so early into the job. It was a matter of time now before they would get paid.

Kenneth held it open for James, then set a triangular block under the door to keep it from shutting. Fool me once, he thought as he wedged the doorstop tight between the door and the carpeted floor.

James went directly behind the counter and plugged the saw in a nearby outlet. The isosceles-shaped nose became a blur, whirring back and forth, as he gave the trigger a test pull. It felt good in his hands. He was more than ready to use it, hungry to destroy, the rush of adrenaline causing his hands to shake with excitement.

Kenneth took the can of spray paint from James' coat pocket, dropped it to the floor, and pushed an enormous audio-visual cart aside side to expose the bare wall. Using the spray can, he marked a red arch tall as he stood and three times as wide.

"That should do it," Kenneth said.

"I'll say," James agreed.

With the nose of the rigid blade firmly against the wall at the peak of the arch, James pulled the trigger. The electric saw immediately jumped back and almost leapt from his grasp. Slightly embarrassed, he tried again. This time he was careful not to hold the trigger down. He leaned his whole body into the tool as he tapped the trigger in short, controlled bursts of energy that allowed the sharp tip to plunge slightly deeper each time. Within a minute, he was able to hold the throttle wide open. The saw efficiently divided the thick plaster rock and the hidden wood studs. In twenty minutes, the wall would be nothing more than rubble.

The machine was loud in the undisturbed silence. Unable to hear anything over the saw's motor, James felt a slap against his shoulder.

"I gotta use the john," Kenneth yelled in his ear.

James shook his head yes, never taking his eyes from his work. The notch-toothed blade devoured the wall. When he reached the floor, he followed the red line to the left and then to the right. Finished with the dust-covered tool, he could still feel the motor still vibrating in his palms as he used the sledgehammer to expose the office on the other side.

There was enough light from the library to see half a dozen computers in the darkened office. Every desk accented with a flat top monitor. James only hoped that they would have enough time to poke through the drawers. There was probably a dozen of those IPods and a couple hundred bucks worth of trinkets stashed. Kenneth couldn't have been more right about this score if he worked here. It was going to take all night to carry all this stuff to the van.

Aggravated, Kenneth still hadn't come back, James went to hunt him down. Lazy asshole, he thought. It was one thing to tear the wall out by himself. It was another to expect him to haul all this shit alone like some kind of goddam mule.

When he pushed the wood, bathroom door open, careful not to put his hand against the shiny brass push-plate, he found Kenneth.

"Jesus H. Christ!" James yelled, his voice echoing off the tiled walls.

Kenneth stood in shock. Not sure what James had said, unsure if he was cursing at him or himself. He knew what he meant though. No two ways about it, they were fucked.

The bald headed man in the gray blazer was dead. A knife with the Swiss Army logo on the handle stuck out from his chest. His eyes were frozen in perpetual surprise unlike the smiling picture that hung from his neck by a lanyard. The insignia of an embroidered library logo over his left breast ironically read *'Know Better.'*

"I was finishing my business, coming back to help you," Kenneth said. "I was going to wash my hands when this guy kicks the door open, holding that knife out. Before he could say boo, I rushed him. All I wanted to do was get by, leave him flat on his ass, but he grabbed me by the throat. We fell on the floor, him on top of me. He did it to himself, man."

James noticed an unusual bulge inside the dead man's coat. Opening the guard's jacket with the toe of his shoe, a dog-eared copy of 'Spider Man's Amazing Powers' fell out.

Kenneth's shirt was crusting in coagulated blood. The red tide had become a sticky, black puddle under the man. Easy money, my ass, James thought.

"What do you want to do now?" James asked.

"Man, let's get the fuck out of here."

"Without the computers? No fucking way."

"I don't know, man."

"You don't know. The hell you say." James stood eye-to-eye with his partner. "Don't you go chicken shit on me now. This is bad, no doubt, but…shit happens. Now deal with it."

***

They worked in silence, disconnecting the computer cables with a pair of lineman's pliers, careful not to cut the power supplies to the hard drives or the monitors. They made trip after trip to the van through the back stairwell, filling the mini-van's ample cargo space. They had planned to use the elevators, but neither could take the idea of having to pass the corpse in the bathroom over and over again.

***

After going back to Kenneth's house for a shower and clean clothes, while his mother bitched the whole time about her having to take the bus to work, they drove to Big Pop's place.

Soft jazz played through a small transistor radio bought new before Kenneth or James had been born. The tortoise shell case had faded over the years, but the sound was as clean as the day Big Pop bought it.

The little bell jingled above the barbershop door. Big Pop sat in his chair, hidden behind his newspaper page. He knew who it was without looking.

"What's up, Pop?" Kenneth said.

"Morning, boys," He said as he laid the newspaper over his lap. "You two read the paper much?"

"No, sir," James said. Kenneth smiled as if Big Pop had recited a favorite joke.

"I guess your generation gets all its information from that Internet."

"Sure, Pop," Kenneth said, "whatever you say. Its been a long night and all I want to do is go to sleep. Where do you want these computers?"

"You can throw them in the Mississippi for all I care."

"Now wait a minute," James said. "We've gone through a hell of a lot of trouble to get these here. You made us a promise."

"True that," Big Pop said, "Of course our deal went dead as disco when that guard got killed."

"What the hell you talking about, Pop?"

"I'm talking about that 'brave guard' who was killed last night, who happens to be the Chief of Police's godson."

He handed the folded newspaper over to them, the smiling picture from the guard's ID badge was in full color, three times bigger for the front page. James mind flashed to the guard lying on the floor, lifeless. The knife embedded in the middle of his chest. A quote from the Chief promised 'quick justice.' James believed him.

"All that work for nothing," Kenneth said.

***

James took the crumpled, dirty bills from his pocket and combined them with the change on the bar. It had been a slow morning. It was always like that after the holidays. People were broke and the suburban guilt that had made him flush had now been replaced by the hangover of credit card debt. He had collected twenty-one dollars in six hours and felt damn fortunate to have done so well.

The bartender moved slowly with his right arm in a sling. He placed a beer next to James' half-empty shot glass, before he leaned against the bar with his good hand.

"How's your pal doing?"

"He's making it. Got lucky. Some big shot lawyer who hates the police took his case. His odds on the needle are still fifty-fifty though."

James swished the hard-liquor around in his mouth letting it burn his tongue and cheeks. The taste always reminded him that life was best if you remembered to enjoy the little things. Anybody could be rich, have nice clothes, a big house, and drive fancy cars. To be truly happy though was priceless.

"Its some kind of world we're living in," the bartender said.

"How so?" James asked.

"Your buddy, the fucking Rams, this shitty economy. This world is going to hell in a handbasket." Without asking, maybe out of habit or kindness, he refreshed James' shot glass. "Know what I'm saying?"

"Brother," James said grateful for the free drink, "It could always be worse."

Free Advice

The sign on the door read 'closed for repairs.' From what I could see, those repairs had ceased to exist. Through the dirty panes of glass, the abandoned store looked beautiful to me.

In my mind I could clearly see it. A rainbow-colored jukebox would sit in the corner. A mahogany bar long as a school bus would serve the house special, a shot and a beer. Bottles of hard liquor would camouflage the mirror behind them and a cash register that relied upon paper receipts, not fallible computer chips would keep accounts square.

The centerpiece would be a pool table. Not one of those unleveled quarter-fed jobs. This would be regal, with claw-feet, and more oak than Grandma's dining room table. Dressed in blood red felt with black leather pockets, a serious game table. It would be for men who played for pride in their neighborhood, not money in their pocket.

It would be the kind of place to grow old in, not rich. The money would be enough to keep the lights on, give-or-take a month, and give me something to do in my twilight years.

When I was young, I had an insatiable appetite for power and money. Before I had graduated college, I already had a thriving store. From my parents' basement, I sold designer knock-offs. I had stole the idea from a guy I'd seen on a trip out East, doing the same thing, instead of a house he used an enormous moving truck.

The women there couldn't get enough. Between the clothes and the people, I could hardly breathe inside those aluminum walls. These women, on the other hand, were like miners working a claim. Carefully studying the dress tags for size, product care, and, most especially name. They knew that those designer names were all forgeries, yet it didn't stop their purchases. If anything it influenced them. The more they coveted the name of some light in the loafer seam-ripper, the more they hoarded, their arms going numb under the garments' weight.

In the Midwest, I knew no self-respecting woman would climb aboard some filthy truck to find the fountain of youth, much less a silk blouse. On the other hand, they had no reservations about coming into a stranger's home, walking among someone's exercise equipment and boxes of Christmas ornaments to find a bargain. It was what I dubbed the 'yard sale mentality.' A frugal code by which I knew these down-to-earth people could relate.

I deliberately asked for twenty percent more than I needed to make a profit. These women loved nothing more than a bargain. It was the idea that they had negotiated the price, 'Jewed me down' as they were so fond of bragging to their friends in giggling whispers.

Occasionally, one of those snobby, West County bitches would come into my store. They would rub the material between their fingers like a booger into a ball. It wasn't a discount they came for as much as to chastise me about how I made my living and the poor indentured servants in third world countries who I helped to keep enslaved. I happily accepted their phony diatribes of inflated morality along with their husband's money.

I met Gloria in that basement. The first time I saw her I knew she was the one. She was a sweet and innocent girl. Whatever I said, despite being a tremendous liar, she accepted at face value. I found her naiveté and beauty impossible to resist. We were married exactly one year after the day we met.

She didn't understand how I made so much money, and I didn't feel any compulsion to tell her. However, when she announced to me after four months of marriage she was pregnant, I knew I had to get serious.

The freedom to make money and not pay taxes had allowed me to accumulate a small king's ransom. In the closet of our one bedroom apartment, I had almost a hundred grand. My biggest problem was cautiously using the money without raising the IRS' suspicions. If their big snouts began rooting through my finances, it would cause a shitload of grief even I couldn't afford.

I called an old friend I knew I could trust with my life. Louie had been the one who had encouraged me to always 'go for it.' We had been drinking buddies and cheating fools the four years we had hung out at Saint Louis University. If we learned anything there it was money buys anything. Lecture notes, term papers, and test answers were funded by the illegal beer bashes we hosted. What's twenty bucks to an eighteen-year-old kid eager to get blitzed? To Louie, and me, it was an income that supplemented all our deviant needs.

Louie said I couldn't have called at a better time. Over drinks, he told me about these guys, the Russo brothers, who had been helping him. Like me, he was making cash hand over fist, but was unable to prove his income to the government. After he put his stake down, he was made a paid consultant. That initial investment, however, was non-refundable.

"Seems like a hell of a lot of money to throw away," I said.

"What's fifty grand, pal? I'll tell you what it is. The cost of doing business. You think if Uncle Sucker finds you have all that script tucked under your mattress, fifty large is gonna satisfy those pricks? Don't be an asshole."

We went to see the Russo brothers the next evening. The dingy, gray shop cluttered with old tires and detached bumpers smelled of oil and brake dust. I felt apprehensive and would have bolted if not for Louie's presence. What if these goombas get busted or can't remember me a week from now or start to blackmail me until I can't pay any more and have to start doing jobs for their bosses? Once I handed the envelope stuffed full of hundred dollar bills over, ironically, my anxiety stopped. We shook hands and the two Russo brothers, encouraged me, saying, "Not to worry 'bout nuffin'."

A year later, life was great. On paper, I didn't have shit. Russo Engine and Transmission repair owned my house and cars. The small commission checks I collected every two weeks, my claimed income, gave the federal ball-busters no reason to investigate my earnings.

Gloria enjoyed shopping, buying anything she or the baby needed. I liked watching the kid learn to walk and giving my wife a fistful of cash every week. I gambled with Louie and the Russo brothers every Tuesday night. At the theater my wife and I sat in the most expensive seats possible. I bought opulent gifts for Gloria's mother while I drank top shelf liquor and smoked twenty-dollar stogies. All the simple pleasures of suburban domesticity that money could buy.

One day, I walked into the Russo's shop, to get my pitiful check and my cash allowance, but nobody was around. My first thought was a robbery. The brothers had been kidnapped and were bleeding to death in the trunk of some rival gang's Cadillac. Then I heard the coughing. Following the hacks, I discovered the brothers huddled over a desk, each with a trimmed down fast-food straw in their noses like a walrus missing a tusk. A pile of coke as big as my fist sat in a mound between their bowed heads.

Without a word, I sat down at the table with them. I intended to wait them out, but the younger Russo cut me a line, and handed me a straw. What the hell I figured, sticking the straw that still smelled of Pepsi into my nostril. The drug's potency hit my brain like an orgasm times a million.

Through a cocaine driven haze, my son began to grow up and I hardly noticed. The little I did come home, Gloria usually met me at the door, furious, wanting to know where I had been, why had I even bothered to come home, and most of all, where was the all goddamn money going?

Little by little, our home disappeared. First to go was the TV and the surround sound system, then the dining room set and Gloria's great-grandmother's china. Not so bad, things that could be replaced if I could cut back, but I couldn't. Next went the living room furniture and our bedroom set. When Gloria came home and found the copper plumbing gone, she took the kid and left. It was a week before I realized it.

When I went to her mother's, she wouldn't open the door. I could see my boy through the curtains, crying to see me, and still, she wouldn't open the door. By the time the cops arrived, I had smashed out the window.

Two days later, as I collected my personal belongings from the sergeant's desk, I was served an emergency order of protection. Given Ex Parte, while I puked my guts out in the city's metal toilet, her attorney had been hard at work. She shouldn't have bothered. I had already made up my mind I wasn't ever going to see her or my son again.

The one thing I still had was my car. I needed cash. I needed coke. I went to the one place that seemed to have a never-ending supply. A mile from the Russo brother's shop, I ran out of gas.

I walked the rest of the way, but wasn't worried. I would go in, get a bump, grab a little do-re-mi, and hit the streets. I knew enough hustlers to find somebody who needed something, and a guy like me who could connect the dots.

The surprise that I got when I saw those chains on the gate was like holding a firecracker too long. You can't believe it happened. But it did.

The IRS had shut it down. An armed guard in a blue windbreaker stood staring at me. He came toward the gate and I ran. I didn't stop until my lungs had shriveled to the size of raisins in my chest. I hid behind a dumpster, trying not to breath. To my surprise, no one had been following me. No hound dogs bayed out my position or cracks of rifle fire flew toward me. Nevertheless, I was scared out of my mind.

I asked myself, 'How the hell could this have happened?' We had been careful, in spite of the drugs. Our books were flawless. Everybody filed their taxes on time and religiously rendered unto Caesar on April fifteenth.

Then it occurred to me. Gloria wasn't a wide-eyed girl anymore. Whether she wanted protection, from me or maybe the Russos, it was hard to tell. If it were her alone, I don't think Gloria would have said shit if she had a mouth full. Her mother and my boy, though, were innocent bystanders. They were the ones who needed protection. The kind the Federal witness relocation program offered like candy from a stranger in a dark sedan. Once you took it nobody ever saw you again.

I went underground with friends for as long as they would suffer me. When they found their kids piggy banks mysteriously empty, checks and credit card statements with huge cash advances they certainly would have remembered, I would leave. Sometimes peacefully, under the cover of night. Sometimes, with a black eye and a bloody lip.

One night, smoking crack in an abandoned downtown loft, I heard about the Russo brothers. How their name came into the conversation as we passed the glass dick in a circle, I can't remember. I do recall losing my buzz immediately when I was told that they were doing twenty to fifty for tax evasion and armed assault on a federal officer. Nobody died but several gold badges found out if their bulletproof vests worked that afternoon.

My son, is a man now, good looking like his mother. I've bumped into him a couple of times at the downtown library. It's a block away from the homeless shelter where I take most of my meals.

The first time I saw him, it paralyzed me. Ten minutes after he left I was still standing in the same spot. I came out of it when the jackoff security guard pushed me out the door. I knew better than to fight him. He was just doing his job, probably no more happy about it than I was.

Now, when I see my son, I cautiously follow him as he regularly reviews the books on how-to-write. I hope that he is a writer, aspiring or otherwise, doing something noble with his life, not looking for the easy way like I did.

"You lose something in there?"

I had been so lost in my dreams of legitimacy that I hadn't seen the cop standing right next to me.

"No officer," I said meekly, careful not to make eye contact.

"Move along," he said, motioning me in the side with his nightstick.

I took his advice. Behind the building in my cardboard squat, I got comfortable. I had missed supper, and my stomach let me know it.

Tomorrow, maybe, I would see my son. That would be nice.

Blackwater Opera

The LED detonator reached quadruple zero. Karen had expected, anticipated excruciating pain, but the moment was the equivalent to a pin's prick. Then she felt nothing. No more pain or joy, no more shame or condensation or fear, no more body or faithfulness to it, and no more servitude to this world. It was not nirvana or heaven or anything she had been promised. A lone sense of floating in weightlessness was all that remained. She could see the explosion billowing in orange and black clouds below her. A wave of sheer energy rippled out turning over cars with the resistance of leaves in the fall and leveling the surrounding buildings without regard for brick or glass.

To Karen's surprise, she heard the faint cry of an infant, then its quieted greedy suckle. Amy was no longer pregnant. Her child, a girl she presumed by the pink swaddling, and she was like Karen, floating above the mass destruction. She noticed the doctor, the nurse, and the security guard. They were holding hands and singing, but she couldn't hear them.

Karen could not feel her body, yet still felt alive. The others around were the same as she had remembered them in the clinic with the exception of Amy, yet even she appeared relatively similar to her pre-natal self. Their clothes were not stained, they were not drenched in blood nor were they screaming in pain.

Without realizing it how it came to pass, she was next to Amy. Karen laid her hand upon the infant's round head, gently stroking the whisper of fine hairs that covered its scalp. The child was beautiful. Karen could feel the baby's warmth and smell its newborn scent. There was no doubt to her that these people, including herself, were dead. An amazing fact she didn't question.

The doctor was first. With the grandiose vigor akin to a bottle rocket, he shot straight up, his only remnant a silver tail briefly visible, then gone. The nurse and security guard did likewise.

"What is her name?" Karen asked sensing Amy's departure next.

"Hope."

"A beautiful name."

Amy's ascension was no less different than the clinic employees, but with her going Karen felt two things: remorse and a sense of falling.

The flames billowed and raged and she fell through them without resistance. Through the roof, the I-beams, the floor, and the concrete she fell and did not stop. What she perceived to be her flesh was pulled from her body with an immeasurable agony. Her exposed red muscles wrapped in blue veins fell away in chunks as the descending acceleration increased. Then those sections ripped away and exposed the white bone that lay beneath. The skeletal features reminded her of the anatomy class figure from her tenth grade science class. She had wondered then about the accuracy of such things. Her bony white fingers connected by cartilage to the forearm confirmed that indeed the model had been correct.

It began with her feet. Unlike a skydiver falling face-first, she was descending with the efficiency of a missile. Karen no longer felt the previous intense pain, but a pins-and-needles sensation that moved up her body. The bone was evaporating, turning to sparkling dust. It reminded her of the special effects used in movies to simulate the whizzing by of stars at incredible speeds.

In a brief flash, she saw her life with the perspective of a narrator telling her life story from the push to exit her mother's womb to the bomb's detonation. Her whole life revealed to her with the secret, omniscient knowledge of what consequences each choice brought and how things could have been different. It was the most wonderful, heartbreaking thing she had ever experienced.

"My God, what have I done?"

The blackness was complete and perfect. No sound or flicker of light to disturb the pure tranquility that it was and Karen without, permission or forgiveness, became the black, then became nothingness itself.

***

Karen walked with her arms folded around herself despite the sunshine that warmed Carondelet Park. It would be easy to mistake her body language as a woman chilled than a person under enormous stress.

She had thought she had come to terms with what had to be done. It wasn't like this happened last night. Her appointment, for which she had volunteered, had come months ago. Karen was proud then to have been selected for "Operation Blackwater," to have been singled out from the group as special, unique in the fact that she could help carry the message to the world.

Karen had found *God's Chosen People* on the Internet by Googling religion plus mysticism. She had skimmed sites that revolved around the Kyballah, the Koran, and several that claimed transcendental meditation through statuary, their human (still living) founders, or the ingestion of drugs. Her interest was peeked though by the GCP's website's fundamental biblical ideology.

They were staunchly independent, stating that all organized religions had been corrupted in the pursuit of money. Salvation, which each claimed alone they could offer, were nothing more than plots to collect wealth, land, and slaves in order to supplement their leaders opulent lifestyles. Karen couldn't have agreed more.

The GCP believed by extracting themselves from the world, from its system of commerce, and the illusion of personal property, could one indeed know true freedom. The true church, the one spoken of in the Book of Revelation, would be uncontrolled by such encumbrances. That through group consciousness, reliant on mass meditation toward its goals they would not only be prepared for the end times, but be crucial in bringing it about.

The end of the world did not concern Karen. Murder, genocide, starvation, droughts, floods, rape, global warming, drug wars, child exploitation were reported so blasé within the allotted ten minutes before sports and weather, she did not have to be convinced that the human race was already damned.

The GCP's website was not an advertisement or incitement for the wayward seeker as much as a declaration of intentions, a notice to the world at large that they had no reservations in regard to fulfilling the 'end times' predictions.

Karen liked this kind of straightforwardness sans the charming commercialized come-ons for peace and tranquillity. It was exactly the kind of thing she wanted. She had thoroughly searched the website for an hour and could not find one crucial element. There was no address or phone number. There was however a tab labeled 'Contact Us.'

The contact page was standard in that it asked for name, address, telephone, and e-mail address. All the regular and expected stipulations of the modern times to which Karen conceded.

After that, it became more like an entrance exam. They wanted to know the odd, intimate details such as age, weight, hair color, eye color, and annual yearly income. All relatively simple to answer with drop-down menus or click and fill dots nostalgic of a SAT answer sheet. Then there were the essay questions.

"Who, in your opinion, is the most relevant figure of the Bible and why?"

"Do you believe in the relevance of fasting to understand God's will?"

"Have you ever sensed or audibly heard God speaking to you?"

Karen answered each in less than a hundred words. She had written three books (all flops) and found it child's play to respond. Blithely she wrote meaningless, politically correct statements that gave away none of her personal character. The last question, however, stopped her stream of consciousness cold.

The question appalled her, yet Karen wanted to answer it. It had come to define her life as before and after. Her fingers trembled on the home-row keys, wondering if she could answer.

"Have you ever had an abortion? If yes, explain."

***

"I'm pregnant," Karen said.

Bobby asked, "How? We were careful."

Silently, she agreed. Karen may have been fifteen but was well enough informed in the use of contraception. It was the nineteen eighties for Christ sake. She had got the pill thanks to the free clinic and had enough rubbers for Bobby to last until Christmas. Between the two items, they should have been bulletproof.

That was until the big party seven weeks ago. Bobby was drunk, she was high, and, shit happens.

"You're sure?" he asked.

Karen wanted to scream. She wanted to tell him three positive EPTs couldn't be wrong. That she didn't know what she was going to do, how she could ever tell her mom and dad, but all that came out was a squeak followed by her uncontrollable tears.

Bobby held her to his chest, her sobs muffled inside his black t-shirt. He understood what this meant and knew there was but one unattractive option. It wasn't like he ever intended on marrying her or that he was in love with her, and he sure as hell wasn't going to pay child support. A kid would fuck up all his plans.

At twenty years old, Bobby was the best drummer in St. Louis. In less than a month, his band would be going to L.A. This bullshit couldn't have come at a worse time. He patted her back with a sure hand soothing Karen with false promises. "It's going to be all right. Don't worry, baby. I'll fix everything."

Karen stopped crying. At rest against her boyfriend's chest she wasn't sure what he had in mind. The comfort of his beating heart in her eardrum drowned out the world and all its problems. If he said it would be okay then she believed him. He had told her many times, late at night post-coitus that he was going to be a rock star. That he would have a mansion and cars and money. She believed every word, and even though he hadn't said it outright, she was certain those plans included her.

It was the next day Bobby picked her up from school in his van. Karen wanted to know where they were going, but he refused to tell her.

"It's a surprise," he said.

She was letdown when they arrived in the unknown driveway. It was attached to a plain, simple house like the others in the subdivision bordering Grant's Farm. She could see the multi-car trolley from the passenger seat slowly roll along, full of tourists and little kids among the wild buffalo.

"This is the surprise?" she asked. Bobby was by far the most exciting person she had ever known.

He introduced her to his friends. He gave her alcohol, weed, and had been her first lover. Bobby had indoctrinated her into the real world. Her life had become a sensational blur of new experiences with him she couldn't have conceived three and a half months ago. Even in her worst times, puking her guts into a toilet, he was there holding back her hair. She trusted him more than any person in her life.

"The surprise is inside," he said.

Bobby was smiling, but it was forced. Not the casual, devilish grin he usually wore. Still, this did not bother her. She believed whatever he had planned would be something to cherish for a lifetime.

Karen walked the short path to the front door holding Bobby's hand. She could hear the bell ring inside and her mind hopefully wandered. Maybe this was his dad's house. She knew Bobby's mother had left when he was little, but he had spoke occasionally about his father. How he believed in him, bought him his first drum-kit at four, and paid for lessons until he was thirteen. That's what this must be. They couldn't get married. Hell, even she knew that, but they could share their secret with somebody who might understand. A man who would in theory adopt her, helping her with the trials that were ahead while waiting patiently for Bobby's return.

The door opened and a man with thick glasses and a bushy gray mustache greeted them. He perfunctorily shook each of their hands, inviting them inside. Karen noticed how filthy his fingernails looked. She tried clumsily to wipe away his handshake by using the backside of her jeans. His appearance was in alignment to his hygiene. The pants he wore were stained, as was his Hawaiian shirt. There was a distinct odor in the home Karen could not place. It was something between falling face first into a pile of dirty laundry and a girl's locker room.

They followed the man through the disheveled rooms, down a flight of creaky wooden stairs, to a dimly lit basement. It was an average suburban romper room full of abandoned, but still useful furniture.

The man and Bobby, as if in rehearsed collusion, cleared boxes and assorted bric-a-brac from a lopsided pool table. A single light hung above it, casting an intense glare over the green felt.

The man sat down in a wheeled office chair at the end where the balls were traditionally racked. Karen could hear the tink of metal against metal and see the occasional brilliant silver flash as the man organized his surgical instruments instead.

Bobby walked over to her and took her hand, leading Karen toward the game table. She followed with no more resistance than a lamb to be slaughtered.

The man instructed her to remove her pants and underwear. Uncertain and modest in the presence of the stranger, Bobby coaxed her. He told not to worry that this guy was a friend and that he wouldn't hurt her.

"Are you sure about this, Bobby?" Karen asked.

Bobby hugged her reassuringly and kissed her gently upon her forehead.

"It'll be over before you know it," he said.

Nude from the waist down, Karen sat with her legs spread before the man with each heel secured inside a leather pocket. Bobby, per the man's instructions, sat behind her, propping her up, but mainly to keep her from moving once the procedure began.

"This might pinch a bit," the man said.

The pain was magnificent. Her groin felt as if had been intentionally set on fire and the man was thoughtlessly injecting her with gasoline.

Bobby was strong and until this moment she had loved that about him. He was relentless in his grip. She was no match for the power either man held over her body.

Twenty minutes later, the man and Bobby helped Karen onto a musty smelling couch allowing her to rest. The pain had nowhere near subsided, making her weak and helpless. The shame of lying on the couch was compounded as Bobby and the man laughed, talking like familiar old friends. The worst though was when she saw her beloved boyfriend paying the man and him counting the bills in his blood-stained hands.

This was nothing more than a business transaction between men and she the debasing reason that brought them together. Before blacking out, she realized she was not special to Bobby, that this wasn't the first time he had participated in such a grotesque party with this man, and how stupid she was for ever thinking that he loved her.

Karen woke in the hospital screaming. The sterile white room was empty. When the nurse came in, she was disappointed that it was not Bobby. The pain was gone, but she felt very different down there.

The nurse was nice and held her hand. She explained how her parents had rushed her to the ER in the nick of time to save her life. She was lucky to be alive after this sort of thing.

"I do have some bad news though," the nurse said. "I'm not really sure if it is my place to tell you or not, but I think if it was me, I would want to know."

"What?"

"The doctors did everything they could dear, but there was so much damage."

Karen knew what she was going to say. Bobby, in his selfishness, had taken from her the one, precious gift all women clung to for redemption.

"You're condition was declared critical. The only way to save your life was a hysterectomy." The nurse paused, then asked, "Do you know what that is, sweetie?"

Nodding her head yes, Karen knew. She had read about it in a book once. Afterwards, the main character lost her mind and killed herself. She had no desire to do likewise, yet the idea of castrating Bobby to level the scales felt well enough.

The nurse held Karen's hand while she cried. Her emotions ran the gamut from loss, to rage, to grief, to humiliation all at once.

"There, there, dear," the nurse said, "everything will be better in the morning."

***

Karen had almost marked the e-mail spam. It had been weeks since her cathartic, honest answer to the question that seemed to control her life. It had felt good to put everything into writing, to re-live it via hindsight.

Hello and felicitations Karen,

You're response has been thoroughly reviewed by the Elder tribunal. It is their unanimous decision that you're heart is without the underlying motives of greed, jealousy, or contempt.

On behalf of the Council of New Souls, we invite you to come as our guest, to sit among us, judge us with the same scrutiny that has been applied to you. As it is written, 'Many are called, few are chosen.'

There is a link attached to this communication. If you should decide to come, please respond to it likewise. If not, then we bid you peace and good will.

All that we ask before you answer is that you would find a quiet place, guaranteed to be free from interruption, and seek God's will. This may be the end of the journey or its sanctified beginning. That alone you must decide.

Sincerely,

Disciple Danielle
Order of Messengers
<u>DDMessenger@Godschosenpeople.info</u>

    She printed a copy, placed it in her purse, and took it with her to work.

    Re-reading the e-mail several times, she evaluated it for the overall content, dissecting paragraphs and phrases. Karen made her best efforts to read between the lines, but couldn't help feeling like she had won something expensive.

    By lunch, she had accomplished little in the way of work. Her normal high volume would offset a non-productive morning such as this. Karen had already surpassed her monthly quota and was certain that after lunch she could get back into the flow of things.

    At noon, she as well as her co-workers stopped their work in unison. No one was allowed to finish whatever precious document he or she found themselves assigned. Furthermore, no one could return to their station and begin working so much as one second before one o'clock. A computer program enforced the strictness. It locked out all users should some incompetent clerk try to sneak back in to meet their quotas. Karen felt sorry for anybody with such desperate thoughts.

Admittedly, times were hard and good jobs like these were difficult to find, but either you had it or you didn't. Every month she would be introduced to a smiling, new face eager to confront the challenge she had found less than demanding for ten years. Karen was a natural born ringer for such mundane work. It suited her fine to sit and type whatever was put on her desk. She never questioned its purpose or principal and at the end of the day, couldn't have told you what she had been privileged to if injected with sodium pentothal. That was usually what made somebody leave. Not the idea of quotas, although it was normally cited as the reason for termination.

Her department strictly transcribed documents from dictation. It was no longer a shock to see a new co-worker bolt upright alarmed. Management gave, at most, one free pass to new hires. Often, a senior manager would have a private meeting with the individual. Afterwards the employee would either leave or suck it up. Not many stayed longer than a year.

Karen was one of four who had been there the longest. The others rarely spoke to her as they had nothing outside of work in common. She didn't mind though. If the roles were reversed, there was no doubt she would have done the same.

Karen left the building and walked to a dedicated greenspace three blocks away. It was generally a hangout for homeless men. At night it was dangerous, but during the Monday through Friday lunch hour it was relatively safe and the bums left her alone.

She ate her plain lunch of peanut butter and honey on toasted wheat bread, washing down the thick sustenance with bottled water. Karen ate slowly and thought about the electronic invitation. She would be forty this year. Outside an associates degree, owning a fuel-efficient foreign car, and her failed attempts at authorship, she had done nothing to prove her life. As she re-read the folded copy, Karen thought maybe these people could show her a way to fill the void.

By the time she walked back to the office she had made up her mind. The joy that came with such a confident, forthright decision reflected in her work. Without effort, Karen doubled her normal speed and by three o'clock had to ask her supervisor for a new work batch. Unimpressed, the office matron handed her a sealed manila envelope marked 'CONFIDENTAL.' Desperate not to arouse suspicion, Karen walked indifferently back to her desk although the excitement of her recent decision made her want to caper like a little girl.

***

Still in her coat and sensible shoes, she answered the e-mail forgetting her keys in the front door's lock. She had explained in an overtly lengthy response that she felt led to visit. After forty-five minutes of writing, editing, and worrying, she clicked the send icon. Aloud, she told herself, "Here goes nothing."

The computer binged before she could go to the door to retrieve her remembered keys. Disciple Danielle had responded informally with a time and address they could meet. The quick response surprised Karen and hoped that she had not wasted all that effort to explain her decision to an auto-mailer.

She disregarded the negative thought and used Map-Quest to get directions. The estimated drive time was twenty-seven minutes. If she left now, Karen could be at the Crestwood location with five minutes to spare. It was made clear to her this was a one-time opportunity, and despite the short notice, should she fail to come or be late, there would not be a second chance.

Certain there wasn't another moment to lose, Karen printed the directions, and rushed to her car forgetting to lock the front door.

***

The address was a mid-sized warehouse located behind the mall. Its plain brown brick façade was interrupted by nothing but a pair of aluminum framed doors. The glass had been tinted black and was impossible to see through. Save for the appliquéd white numbers in stark contradiction to the doors, Karen would have had not believed this was the headquarters for God's Chosen People.

A lone, thin woman with a militant style hair cut stood outside smoking. Whether this was Disciple Danielle wasn't clear. It was certain though, she had been waiting for Karen.

Before she was halfway to the doors, the woman was hurrying over to greet her. It was reassuring. She had caught every damn red light Watson Road had to offer and found herself constantly behind the slowest drivers. Karen had parked in the spot designated for 'Visitors' with four minutes to spare. She had thought she had blown it until this lithe woman came to her, embraced her, and never let her go, guiding her from her car through the double doors.

Inside, a deliberate blackout was enforced interrupted exclusively by candlelight. There wasn't a single electric light being used although Karen could discern air conditioning regulating the temperature. The sudden coolness in conjunction with the candles soothed her body and mind.

"Thank you for coming," a woman's voice spoke to her in the dimness. "I am Disciple Danielle."

The woman who had greeted her so lovingly in the parking lot passed possession of Karen's hand to the other woman. Disciple Danielle took an immediate hold, replacing the small woman's hand with her more bountiful flesh.

The small woman clasped her free hands together and bowed in reverence toward them. Karen realized she didn't even know the small woman's name before she was gone somewhere into the dimness.

Visibility, at best, was ten feet in any direction. It was exciting and surreal as the Disciple Danielle led her using the calm strength of her grip and her delicate, whispered voice.

"Now is the hour of meditation. The community is focusing on one thought, as prescribed daily by the Congress of Intercession. Today our singular focus is to project a harmonious tone that will interrupt the world economy tomorrow."

Karen found it a lofty goal, but more reasonable than world peace.

They passed through long corridors. Disciple Danielle didn't seem to need any light to find her way. Karen was grateful for the companionship. She didn't consider herself claustrophobic, but under these circumstances, she couldn't have moved an inch alone.

Occasionally, they did pass others. Small gatherings of men and women, holding hands, and sitting crisscross applesauce. They seemed normal as she, dressed in casual office attire, resting comfortably on oversized cushions. She hadn't known what to expect, yet found the group meditations a welcome shock. It was the kind of peace Karen had been seeking her entire life.

Disciple Danielle suddenly stopped. They seemed to have reached a dead end, the nearest light twenty feet behind them, ahead nothing but blackness. When Disciple Danielle released her hand, she almost cried out in fear.

"Now is the time of your choice," Disciple Danielle said. "You alone must go forward, through the darkness. If you are one of us, you will make it. If you are not, no harm will come to you, but your time here will have been worthless. Do you understand?"

There was a time in Karen's life when she would have turned around, running to find the building's exit. She remembered those people meditating, how serene they seemed to be. If she had to do this, she reasoned, then they did too.

"I do," Karen said.

"Fair thee well, traveler," Disciple Danielle said and was gone, presumably back the way they had come, possibly watching her from a distance. Either way, Karen was alone, barely able to see behind her, and absolute darkness in front of her.

She took a deep breath before she walked forward. The sound of her breath escaping her body masked the pounding inside her chest. A cold sweat chilled her brow and back.

With her arms held out before her, she walked. It was a genuine surprise to her senses that what she had presumed to be a wall directly in front of her was a curtain. A heavy, velvet material that divided as she passed through it. The instant privacy consumed all her senses. She could not see any longer and her hands, though they reached out, felt nothing. Her feet though were still on the same level ground as when she entered. A small comfort to be sure but reaffirming enough.

On the cusp of becoming an emotional wreck she walked in shuffling, tiny baby steps. The deprivation to her senses was taking a toll. She was sure if she called out for help, she would be rescued, but at what cost? If she overcame, then maybe, finally, her life would have a rejuvenated meaning, something beyond meaningless physical or emotional pleasures. A life of which she was in control and not at its' mercy.

A tiny dot of light caught her attention. In a charge, she hurried toward it, and fell skinning the palms of her hands. Karen disregarded the pain, stood up, calmed down and started again. Her gait now was a determined, slow stride. She concentrated on the light, wanting it more than anything she ever had before. It occurred to her that this might be insanity, like the illusion of an oasis in the desert. Madness be damned, she thought. It was the only hope she had and she clung to it.

The hole was tiny, but in the darkness, even the slightest light is brilliant. Karen peered through the small opening. Unable to see clearly, she leaned her head as close to the puncture as possible. Karen lost her balance and fell forward, splitting a pair of drapes identical to the ones she had entered through. Determined not to sustain another scraping to her already raw palms, she regained her poise.

Karen was in awe. She had come out into a beautiful Zen garden complete with fountains, burning incents, bouquets of hanging flowers, koi ponds, and a small bridge leading to a chair engraved with the sun and moon headrest. The beauty and serenity was her fantasy come true.

***

In the following weeks and months, Karen thrust herself into all things relevant to the GCP. She read dozens of books on meditation, enlightenment, and the origin of the soul. The subject she found most fascinating though was transcendental meditation. This idea of traveling outside of your body to explore distant places, able to go back and forth in time was astounding. Unlike drugs, there were no residual effects, and it became better each time she experimented with it.

Then, of course, was the tenet to shed worldly possessions. Karen gladly gave away her TV, DVD player, and most of her furniture. With permission from the Jury, she was allowed to retain her bed and car. The hardest thing to give up was her precious laptop. It had been a lifeline for so long it was like turning her back on a close friend.

At work, her concentration faltered to dangerously low levels. She could no longer ignore what she was doing. Writing letters for ball-buster corporate attorneys threatening frivolous lawsuits, that if perused, would destroy their lesser opponents. Memorandums thick as small books outlining the acquisition and dissemination of corporations that would leave hundreds unemployed. Debt collection manuals that instructed operators on how to properly design re-affirmation agreements to restore discharged balances with usury rates certain to repeal any assistance issued by the bankruptcy court.

Is this what she had been doing with a decade of her life? In a futile attempt to keep her newfound serenity, she asked for re-assignment to anywhere else in the company. Upper management issued a quick, thoughtless denial followed in kind by a written reprimand. She was warned that if she continued with such reckless behavior, her termination would be imminent.

Karen took her problem before the Elder Tribunal. They concurred that she had achieved a significant state of enlightenment, and her place was strictly among her own kind. If she so wanted, they would foster her matriculation to discipleship, if in exchange she would renounce all her worldly ties. Without hesitation, Karen agreed.

In a matter of twenty-four hours, Karen sold her car, abandoned her one bedroom studio apartment, and moved with nothing but the clothes on her back into the GCP campus. She had thought about calling work, to inform them of her decision, but decided that it would only continue to support the negative energy they manufactured. It was best to make it a clean break, free of any encumbrances, to have no barriers by which her enlightenment could be swayed.

Alone that evening in her assigned room, an indistinguishable cell from the rest of the community, Karen found peace. She had no worries. Everything from this point on would be provided, as she needed it.

**

Karen received her rank as Disciple one year to the day she entered the private cooperative. Without the distractions of the outside world her ability to excel had no limitations.

With rank came privilege, and she was granted access to a manual typewriter. She wrote several documents cataloguing her transcendental travels that were eventually compiled into a two-volume work upon the recommendation of her master. It was a great honor, much more than Karen could have ever hoped for in her past life. Here, she was a rare flower allowed to bloom and reveal her beauty. She could have gone on living this way into infinity.

Asleep, her master woke her.

"Disciple Karen," he said loudly, "you need to rise immediately."

Instantly awake, she put on her shoes. A true disciple never questioned their master. She was curious though as to why she was so urgently needed.

She stood to face him as he placed both his hands on her shoulders, his joy undeniable. "The Great Ones have called your name. You have been chosen to carry out the Supreme Commission."

Karen understood in full what this meant and pretended to be as happy as her master did. She presumed for her lone disobedience, praying that the thing should not come to pass in her tenure, the universe had singled her out.

***

While the coordinated efforts of "Operation Blackwater" where underway nationwide, Karen trained twelve hours a day for her role in the effort. It was boot camp like drills of physical training, nutritional supplication, small arms instruction, thermodynamics, and self-defense tactics.

The Fifty, as they were referred to, had but one opportunity to accomplish their mission. Each person would not be told the location of their target until returned to their individual communities. It would insure against the possibility of even the slightest information leak.

Karen, in spite of her personal reservations, embraced the program. She did well in all areas, but found a particular intuitiveness for explosives. Rapid decomposition and development of high pressures were akin to her theories on OBE's (out-of-body-experiences) and she believed proof of the transcendental argument. If she had more time, she could write down what she now understood and convince the Elder Tribunal to avoid this irrevocable solution. Then again, who was she to question their wisdom? If the time was now, then what choice did she have?

***

The community had taken on a transformation in Karen's absence. She hardly recognized the inner dwelling she had called home.

There was no more library filled with sacred GCP texts. No more meditation garden. The daily ritual seeking oneness with the universe seemed a forgotten ideology. It had become a world of the barest necessities. Hundreds of folding beds littered the Great Hall. Bare bulbs burned incessantly and people, many of which Karen had never seen before, aimlessly wandered. The plain hot meals of oats, rice, and vegetables had all been replaced with surplus food that needed no heat or water.

Karen found it hard to accept. This place for so long had been her sanctuary, a refuge that could not be disturbed. Now it was nothing more than a weigh station that the world would discover soon enough. It saddened her yet renewed her determination to her mission.

***

The newsroom was in a state of flux. People hurried in every direction to answer phones and review the incoming data for even the slightest new information. It was Columbine, Timothy McVey, and Jonestown rolled into one. All other coverage had been suspended. The station dedicated itself to around-the-clock coverage as had every other cable news station. Nobody wanted to be caught doing a filler piece on erectile dysfunction, as another major piece of the story became public knowledge. Until this thing was settled, they would be caught in that continuous loop repeating the story over and over again as the screen filled with horrifying pictures of the dead, the dying, and the destruction God's Chosen People had extracted on this earth.

A man behind a camera pointed to a well-dressed newscaster at a desk. The newscaster had had the good taste to allow his beard to grow in slightly to show empathy with the audience. In his dressing room, he had liked the handsome appeal he felt the dark stubble lent.

"And in five, four, three, two…"

"Good morning nation. I'm Hugh Engle and as this crisis grips our republic, more information continues to come to light in what is being called the largest, most well organized terrorist action ever constructed.

"We go now live to Berry White in Crestwood, St. Louis, with the latest at what is considered to be this nefarious organization's headquarters."

"Thanks, Hugh," Barry said.

Assured by his cameraman they were clear, Hugh pulled out his cell phone to call his agent. They both have been waiting for an opportunity like this to sell him to one of the major networks.

"The bodies were discovered shortly after four a.m. by the ATF serving a no-knock search warrant. After using a tank to crush in the front doors, agents swarmed the building, but found no resistance. However, inside they did find hundreds dead, victims of a mass suicide. At this point, autopsies are being performed on the multitude of corpses, trying to verify the cause of death. We don't have an exact body count at this moment, but it is estimated to be in the hundreds. Tractor-trailers and buses have been converted to transport the massive fatalities. We have been told some of the dead did die from self-inflicted injuries, but authorities refused to elaborate.

"The cult known as God's Chosen People is being held responsible for a death toll estimated in the thousands and damages in the millions. A doomsday cult who believed themselves personally responsible for initiating the biblical prophesies according to the last chapter of the bible better known as Revelation. It is by this action they had hoped to break open what is considered the first seal, bringing forth judgment upon the wicked in preparation toward the Second Coming of Christ.

"In an unprecedented action Christian, Jewish, and Muslim leaders have asked that peace be observed amongst their various factions. The whole world grieves in stunned and saddened silence at the atrocity committed here in St. Louis and the various cities around the world."

Berry's face disappears and is replaced by his voice alone. It narrates over stock footage that has rolled non-stop as filler in-between the live feeds. The dumb luck to have gotten stuck at Lambert Airport when the story broke was now pure gold. If he hadn't missed his connecting flight while he gambled at the Casino Queen, he would have been in the air and shit out of luck. All things considered, it had to be the best three grand he ever lost.

Family Business

Mark stood admiring himself in the mirror. The fog from the shower still outlined the glass, providing a frame to his self-portrait. His hair was still thick and luxurious, black as it had been when he was a young man. A belly, large as a mature pumpkin, stuck out from his mid-section. Despite smoking two packs of menthol cigarettes a day, his teeth were still a phosphorus white.

He dressed in his normal uniform. A filthy white t-shirt, long-sleeved plaid shirt with a pack of cigarettes in the left-hand pocket, and blue jeans seized tight by an unseen belt. The exposed bottom flesh of his stomach, bulbous and hairy, stuck out like a fat lip. Equally, his blue jeans could not fully cover his ass crack.

Rosarita called from downstairs, "Mark, you're going to be late for work."

He ignored her as he huffed and puffed to put on his socks. He caught his breath from the effort in between drags of a cigarette. The black Nikes he wore were kept laced and tied to avoid further strain. Finished with his third cigarette since his shower, he slipped into them like house shoes.

In the full length-dressing mirror, he approved his appearance. As he drew a small, plastic comb through his thick mane, he could still see the young man. The cocky, twenty-something fellow that feared nothing and who had been reckless for the thrill. That young man still lived somewhere deep inside him, protecting him from old age.

A cell phone, not much bigger than his Zippo, vibrated and scooted across the dresser. He knew who it was without having to look at the caller ID.

"I'll be right down," Mark said. There was no need to waste time with pleasantries. Besides, the person on the other end probably wasn't listening anyway.

From his underwear drawer, Mark removed a banded stack of one hundred-dollar bills. He split the cash in half and placed the folded money equally into his front jean pockets. On the off chance Rose might call he decided to take the cell phone.

The truck waited faithfully at the curb. Mark could see Kevin impatient behind the wheel. He consciously slowed. In their work, eagerness was a hazard that could be discerned as nervousness. The people they were going to visit interpreted such ticks as highly suspicious.

The hinges on the truck's metal door groaned desperate for grease. Mark closed the door with a slam and adjusted the springs until they felt comfortable under his ass cheeks.

He lit a cigarette, slightly out of breath, as he changed the radio station from alternative to classic rock. He always did that. Made any environment his. Whether he had permission to or not.

Relaxed, his arm resting on the sill of the open window, Mark was now ready.

Kevin looked at him. He often had to remind himself why in the hell he was doing this. Then he remembered Mark's beautiful daughter. The more excuses he could make to be close to the father, the closer he could be to the daughter. He was ashamed he had masturbated so often to her image and gone as far as to steal her soiled panties to charge his fantasies. The lust he felt was overwhelming, all consuming, debilitating, and wonderful.

"You're early," Mark said.

"Always," Kevin said.

The automatic transmission clunked into drive and the truck lurched forward. Kevin intentionally goosed the accelerator to hear the tires screech. The futility of having to stop fifty feet later never discouraged him. They connected with the highway and drove ten miles-an-hour above the speed limit. Kevin's truck, by no means a sleek racing vehicle, smoothly passed the lunchtime commuters with the immunity afforded to people unaccountable to a company time clock.

Neither man had been legally employed for several years. To them, the idea was preposterous. Legitimate work was for suckers who didn't know any better.

Kevin drove the streets with care after they exited the highway. This was middle-class country. The over-vigilant county police, unlike the city brothers in blue, needed little encouragement. Despite his arrogant attitude toward all authority, Kevin made certain to make full and complete stops, use his turn signals, and never exceed the posted speed limits that changed with every street.

The house was identical to all the others in the subdivision. Perfect square lawns without as much a dandelion to mar the landscape. Every home a mini-tribute to the new wealth spurred by the Internet dot com boom.

Kevin drove the truck slowly into the stain-free driveway. Mark lifted his arm in what might have been viewed as warm salutation to a man on the porch. The man, a sentry, returned the salute and pressed a remote control to open the garage door.

Another man stood inside, a virtual twin of the porch soldier, directing them to advance with hand signals. They sternly obeyed his crisp arm movements, reminiscent of a military police officer, and stopped when ordered by his double closed fists. Kevin and Mark waited until the door shut behind them before stepping out.

The garage's new darkness was strange from the all-engulfing sunshine outside. They both needed a moment to adapt to the nocturnal conditions. Brief as it was, the man who spoke only with his hands, seemed impatient for them to follow.

Inside the house, country music played softly through invisible speakers. It wasn't the upbeat new stuff that was, save the singing style, modern pop music. This was the stuff of whiskey-bottle fueled regret that begged the listener to share the singer's pain.

Buzz sat behind a great oak desk, answering e-mail, looking like a work-from-home yuppie. If not for his stark bald cranium, his sleeveless undershirt deliberately worn to display his tattoos, and the Nazi flag on the wall, he was as suburban as his neighbor's Volvo.

"Que pasa, amigo?" Kevin asked making use of the first-year high school Spanish.

"Nothing much, Holmes," Buzz said looking up from his computer. The litany of people who had stood in front of his desk no longer surprised him. These two, who looked as if they couldn't afford to pay the rent, were no different from those who wore suits or leather jackets. He treated everyone with an unmitigated fairness. As long as they had the cash, he had the time. Buzz would suffer no fools.

"How's business?" Mark asked only making conversation. He sat in the one other chair the office supplied and lit a cigarette. The idea of poisoning by second-hand smoke was not taken seriously within these walls. Ashtrays lay everywhere. Mark placed a multi-faceted glass one on his lap to ash in. It specifically reminded him of one his mother had used until the day she died.

Buzz sucked white smoke through an arm-length water bong. Courteously, he extended the pipe toward Kevin.

"No thanks, bro. I got a long drive ahead of me," Kevin said

With a casual shrug of his shoulders, Buzz took his hit for him. Barely able to see the two visitors through the cloud of carcinogens, "Business is good. It's always good. What can I do you for?"

Mark set the ashtray down, but kept his cigarette between his lips. In a struggle with his body mass, he removed the thick folds of cash.

Buzz let out a low whistle and fanned out the repetitive bills across his desk.

Kevin licked his lips then wiped the saliva from his mouth. He was never sure how much his partner would be carrying, such details were irrelevant, but this much was a surprise. Even to him.

Buzz carefully separated each bill. When he had finished, the shiny glass countertop of his desk was hidden underneath the green rectangles. A coy smile belied the skinhead's satisfaction with the great amount.

"You getting ready for a war or something?" Buzz asked.

"Something like that," Mark said.

"None of my business. Sorry I asked."

Kevin and Mark followed Buzz downstairs.

***

The subterranean coolness seemed even more so in the darkness. Buzz slid his hand over the unfinished drywall and flipped on the lights. The overhead fluorescent tubes tinked and popped from the low temperature inside the frosted glass. As the bulbs warmed the room grew brighter.

Buzz walked ahead not needing the light. When the strobe effect ceased and the dull hum of the lights harmonized, Buzz stood cross-armed in the middle of the basement. Like a proud father, surrounded by the multitude that is his family, he was confident in what he had to offer.

Guns of every fashion filled the room. Rows of shotguns stood in every size and in a variety of colors from camouflage to pink. Rifles were stacked like cords of wood, separated by caliber, their muzzles sticking out as if gasping for air. Handguns of every species, from six shooters to automatic sprayguns, covered and bowed the folding tables where they laid. The smell of gun oil and gunpowder was as intoxicating as a bouquet of fresh cut flowers.

Mark opened his wallet and handed a carefully folded paper to Buzz.

He read the handwritten note silently to himself then called for his helper. Like a ghost, the man seemed to suddenly appear. The helper stood straight as a nail as Buzz read aloud from the sheet.

The servant moved efficiently among the guns with a makeshift shopping cart constructed from a furniture dolly and a oversized crate. He presented the full load for Buzz's inspection.

"Muy bueno, senor. El camion de carga, por favor."

An hour later Kevin and the helper secured a tarp over the truck's bed. The guns and ammunition weighted it down until the axle almost touched the ground. Mark and Buzz placed magnetic signs on either side of the truck, tossed a few shovels and wooden handled rakes atop with several bags of cheap grass seed, and the disguise was complete. Why should the police have any suspicion of a couple of landscapers, slowly plodding along to their next job?

Inside the cab, Kevin turned over the truck's heavy-duty V8 motor. The roar was deafening inside the two-car garage.

As they backed out to the street, Buzz wished them well. "Vaya con Dios, mis amigos." Before they left the subdivision, Buzz counted the cash one more time and locked it in his office floor safe.

***

They plodded along slowly, west to east, deliberately using the inter-connecting streets. The respectable forty-five minute trip to Buzz's place would be a snail's pace two-hour return drive. The main mitigating factors: stop signs and traffic.

St. Louis, per capita, had the most stop signs of any city in America. Kevin dutifully, yet begrudgingly, stopped at every damned one. The last thing he needed was to aggravate some piggy's snout, be pulled over, and find what lay beneath that tarp. If making full and complete stops, painfully resisting the urge to slow and go, could keep him from seeing the inside of a jail, he would do it.

They drove parallel to the highway, through the ruins of old St. Louis. Large homes of all brick, once beautiful were now shells that crumbled from neglect. Enormous factories that had employed thousands were now idle without a solid window left. It was a wasteland that had abandoned all hope. The trade for cheap overseas labor ironically lost more than it had saved.

Mark almost spit his cigarette out when his phone buzzed against his chest. He fumbled with the tiny device dropping and catching the phone in mid-air.

"Hello? Hello? Who is this?" Mark asked.

"Daddy, it's me. Can you hear me, Daddy?" Rose asked.

"Yes, pumpkin," Mark said.

Mark saw Kevin in his peripheral vision pretending not to eavesdrop. It delighted him that Rose would have nothing to do with him. She was seventeen, still a girl consumed with make-up and clothes. In two more months' time, Kevin would become a thirty-year-old man ancient as the dinosaurs, pyramids, and record players to her modern world of MP3s, IMs, and BFFs.

Mark spoke in intimate, hushed tones, deliberately not letting Kevin hear as much as one word of his conversation. He told his daughter he loved her before he closed the phone and replaced it in his shirt pocket.

"Was that Rose?" Kevin asked.

Curiosity killed the cat. The poor bastard's got it bad, Mark thought.

He remembered how he suffered his wife's father. Every Saturday, he listened to the same stories, week after week, nursing his one beer to the old man's dozens. Rosarita, as desperate as Mark was to escape to the darkness of his car, to the secret places youth keeps for virgin lovers, she brought her father beer after beer. Some nights, the old timer went down without a fight, anesthetized by the alcohol. Others, he would find no peace. He would punch walls, break pictures, and push Mark around and sometimes hit him. Out of respect, he never hit back. The man was drunk and should not be held accountable under his own roof.

When Rosarita eventually became pregnant, he did the honorable thing, and asked her father's blessing. After the old man hit him hard across the jaw, almost knocking him unconscious, he embraced him. They drank together all that night, Rosarita served Mark exclusively, sitting on his lap, waiting only for his next command.

This Kevin, he thought, would have no such luck.

"You like Rose, don't you?" Mark asked.

The guilt turned Kevin's face red.

"I thought as much."

Kevin had no words. He kept his eyes forward and concentrated on the road, keeping a look out for cops. Whether he denied or affirmed the accusation, there was no hope. Mark had him dead to rights. Inevitably, he would either let it go or change the subject. If he had learned anything about Mark in the past three years, it was that he had a crippling short attention span. It's why he always drove. One minute, Mark would be lucid, driving with perfectionism a DMV instructor would envy. The next he was everywhere, like a drunk feeling the road to get home, obsessed with fine tuning the radio or lost in some intimate thought.

The halfway point of Natural Bridge was a welcome sight. Rush hour traffic was beginning to form. Long yellow busses intertwined with tiny Japanese cars. People eager to go back home found no solace.

Kevin's truck entered into this busy world unnoticed. Theirs was just another slow-moving vehicle, another target drawing commuter anger. Sometimes, usually a man, would pull along side to stare hard at them. It meant nothing, yet it was always funny to Mark and Kevin. If it tipped the scales back to even, then so be it.

"Mr. Badass there," Mark said as he refused to look over and engage in childish staring games, "if he knew our little secret, eh?"

Kevin agreed, also refusing to look over. They were mules, not murderers or heroes. The light would change, this idiot would peel out proving nothing to them, and they would safely and steadfastly continue.

The blue and white sign declaring 'U-Store It' hovered above them. A chain link fence on rollers slid away after Kevin entered a secret four-digit code. The roll-up, safety-orange colored doors grew larger as the numbers stenciled above them increased. Kevin ignored the addresses as familiar to him in this cubicle maze as in his own neighborhood.

Mark unlocked the door to the storage unit and lifted it high above his head. Kevin parked the truck, then helped Mark close the door, re-locking it from the inside.

The two men worked in silence. They unloaded the guns, sorting and organizing as they went, careful not to accidentally pull a trigger. In their trade, carelessness was how men got killed. Finished, they took the signs off the side of the truck, threw them in back with the other impostures of working men and headed for Mark's house.

***

The truck rested at the curb once again. Neighbors who had been at work earlier were now home mowing grass and washing cars. Children played lively outdoor games or rode bicycles untroubled by their parent's woes.

Rose sat on the porch. On a table, two freshly opened beers waited.

"This was a good day," Mark said.

"Beats the hell out of working for a living," Kevin said.

Rose stood and hugged her father before he sat with his beer. Assured he was comfortable for the moment, she went inside.

Kevin stood and stared at the door holding his beer without drinking. "I love her."

Mark waved his cigaretted hand as if annoyed by a mosquito. It was a foolish thing, this talk of love, he thought. A word used with such carelessness that Mark still wondered at the breadth of its meaning.

"I do," Kevin said.

"You don't know anything," Mark said.

"I know I want to marry her, make her my wife."

"Shut-up."

"No."

"Shut it or I will shut it for you."

"I love her and want to do right by her."

Rose came out, tears in her eyes, slow moving past her father, careful into Kevin's embrace. Her black doe-like eyes pleading for her father's mercy.

"I don't under---"

Kevin placed a loving hand over Rose's stomach, below her navel. Rose placed hers on top of his, trying to smile and not cry, but failed.

Mark sat dumbstruck. He supposed Rosarita already knew.

Road to Hell

Steve rolled off Jeannie, reached across to the nightstand and set a glass ashtray between them. He lit a cigarette for her, then one for himself. The cool menthol burn always tasted good after vigorous sex. In bed, he watched the smoke entrails intertwine, float above, and cling spirit-like to the ceiling.

Sundays, from eight until eleven was their time, while his wife and children attended services. In three weeks, he realized it would be his and Jeannie's second anniversary.

He liked the fact he had a mistress. He loved Brenda and hadn't any plans of abandoning their marriage. Brenda was a good woman. She helped him build his small business from a magnetic sign on the side of his worn out Chevy S-10 into a middle-class income.

In a sense, it was how he met Jeannie. He had searched the steep grade for her blue and white trailer. All these single-wide shanties looked the same to him. Finally, the angular, stick-on number eleven appeared, and he pulled his oversized van into her pea-gravel driveway.

She called him because her kitchen and bathrooms sinks refused to drain. The water was black and stagnant. A seasoned pro at such mundane things, he had a fairly good idea the problem lay somewhere between trailer's discharge pipe and the sewer.

He unloaded a hammer drill and the used tire where he kept the drain snake coiled, then went to work. Under the trailer, he found the clean out. With a large pipe wrench he opened the sealed cap. He hadn't anticipated it being so easy to turn and was immediately drenched in wastewater. The smell was overpowering, but something familiar that no longer made him gag.

Steve attached the steel quarter-inch cable to his drill. He was running forty feet out when the auger bit and twisted viscously in his grip. Automatically he let off the trigger, flipping the slide marked forward to reverse. Steve slid the snake tenaciously warring against the blockage. When he was certain the obstruction had been cleared, he replaced the drain cap and carried the heavy equipment back to his truck.

In the bill, he charged for everything he could think. Residential trip charge, plus inspection fee, plus equipment usage fee, plus hazardous removal fee then added in for time and labor.

Covered in black-speckled filth, Steve knocked on Jeannie's door. She had changed from her initial sweats to Daisy Duke shorts that exposed her ass cheeks and a t-shirt, knotted to reveal her firm belly and accent her small breasts. They both stared at one another, gawking. Wordless, Steve passed the bill to her.

"Damn," she said, "that's a hell of a lot more than I expected."

Steve was used to it. He was almost immune to the shocked reactions his bills affected. It was more a disappointment to him if a customer was happy to pay than not. He was more than ready to recite by rote as to how the bill was calculated according to the duties that were necessary to be performed, the variables that constituted labor, and his closing argument that a professional plumber would have charged triple. Before he could say a word, Jeannie caught him off guard.

"You stink."

"No shit, lady," Steve said "I've been laying in dirt, cobwebs, and feces for the last hour, working on your goddam drain."

"Is it fixed?"

"Yeah, it's fixed."

"What was wrong?"

"You really want to know?"

"Yeah. Was it a rat? We got rats bigger than fucking housecats out here."

"It was your tampons," Steve said. The more she talked the more he was getting pissed. He was usually more gentile with such news, but he could tell she was stalling. To hell with the miss and ma'm shit, he thought, for Christ's sake. Write a fucking check already.

"Oh shit," she said. A smile lit up her face and she couldn't stop from giggling.

Certain she was completely off her nut, Steve pushed the bill. "Lady," he said, "I'm tired. After I get back home and clean up, I still got to take my kid to his t-ball this game. So, if you wouldn't mind…"

"Seeing as you fixed the plumbing, you might as well use it."

"Excuse me?"

"Why don't you come inside and take a shower. I got soap and about a dozen different shampoos."

"I don't know---"

"I could even wash your clothes while you wait."

Steve thought about it. He had a change of work clothes he kept in the van. This wasn't the first time he had been baptized in excremental waters. The image of him changing clothes in his van, shoving the dirties into shopping bags, and the forty minute ride back home reeking of sewer filth wasn't appealing. What the hell, he thought.

He went to the van and grabbed the bag of extra clothes. Before coming inside, he sat on the second-to-last stair tread to remove his boots. In his stocking feet, he walked inside, while Jeannie held the screen door open for him.

"I appreciate this," he said, "but it ain't gonna change that bill none. I've got a family to feed, you know."

"Of course not," she said. "Use the shower in my bedroom. You'll pass the washer on the way. Leave your clothes there and I'll put 'em in."

"Don't bother. Anything you wash is gonna smell for a week later if you do," Steve said. "Put 'em in a garbage sack and throw it out the door. I'll get it when I leave."

"Whatever. Don't make a bit of difference to me."

The shower was small. Jeannie hadn't been kidding about all the shampoo she collected. After sniffing a majority of them, he decided on one that smelled the least like flowers. He wished he had brought some, but how the hell could he have known? The shampoo he normally used looked like tar and smelt worse than vapor rub. It was guaranteed to kill lice, mites, and the whatnot. With all the bacteria he got slimed in regularly, he relied on the medicinal detergent to help keep him healthy. At twenty-two bucks a damn bottle, it better work.

After the shower he felt better. In his line of work, cleanliness was a rare and beautiful thing. Using her brush, he combed his shoulder-length hair. Still black without a hint of gray and thick as bears hide in winter. Observing his physique in the mirror, he wasn't a pound heavier than the day he graduated high school. His body did, however, show the results of his strenuous labors in the form of raised veins and rock hard muscles. It was pleasing to him. While most of his drinking buddies were fat slobs who looked years older than they were, he was often mistaken for thirty when he would soon be eight years older than that in April.

A towel tied about his waist, he opened the bathroom door. Naked and spread eagle on the king-sized bed, Jeannie was unabashedly masturbating herself with a purple vibrator. Steve instantly became erect. With no more hesitation than a dog in heat, he mounted her.

After coming twice, he was spent. He got dressed and stood before her again in his socks. Steve couldn't believe his good luck. Without a care in the world, he tossed his empty gymbag over his shoulder and told her good-bye.

It wasn't until he was outside re-lacing his boots that he thought about it. He forgot to get the check. How the hell could he possibly go back in and ask for money now? The sneaky bitch, he thought.

He picked up a white trash bag he presumed by the smell and weight to be his soiled clothes. Pissed off he had been so gullible, he stopped dead in his tracks. Underneath his driver side wiper blade was a check. In the note field Jeannie had written *For Services Rendered*.

Jeannie still lay in bed as Steve got out. She had lit another cigarette and had turned on the television. It was one of those remodeling shows where in half an hour they turned a shithole into the Garden of Eden. Steve liked that they didn't show the crew of thirty people doing the actual labor. Steve had repaired many a broken pipe by an under-informed do-it-yourselfer. An amusing thought crossed his mind that he should send in a suggestion to the station to do more shows regarding plumbing. It would be good for his business.

The bathroom door closed, Steve turned the shower 'HOT' valve wide open. When the steam had begun to fog the mirror, he tested the water with the tips of his fingers. Slowly, he opened the 'COLD', trying to perfect the water's temperature. When it seemed he was close he stepped inside cubicle closing the white glass door. The water was still too hot and scalded his feet. He added more cold water and the sting subsided. With the removable showerhead he had installed in hand, Steve liberally sprayed his entire body. In ritualistic fashion he moved the water from his groin to his head, as he always had, with no more thought than as to how he ate or sat.

The water was barely tolerable. One degree hotter and he might risk a third degree burn. Steve's theory was whatever micro-bacteria might have attached to him could not survive the elevated heat in conjunction with his energetic scrubbing. It was based in theory to a story his grandfather had told him as a teen-ager.

***

The old man had been in the Navy in WWII. As soon as they docked and were issued liberty, him and his buddies would hit the 'shore-whores.' After four months out at sea, surrounded by swinging dicks night and day, unless you were a sissy, you couldn't wait to dip the ol' wick as soon as possible. A lot of his buddies would stay overnight in the cathouses, too drunk and exhausted to make it back to the ship. His grandfather said he always came back and immediately took the hottest shower he could possibly stand. He claimed, due to this ritual, he was able to avoid the myriad of venereal diseases his buddies suffered.

***

Steve shut off the shower. His skin pink and warm to the touch, he gently patted his skin dry. Jeannie's terri-cloth towels were rough and itchy. Maybe he would buy her some of those good ones he had seen shopping with Brenda. If they were still on sale he would go back and get her a set. If not, then he would buy only one for his exclusive Sunday usage.

Finished attending to his hair, teeth, and under arms, Steve stepped nude back into the bedroom. Searching through his red gymbag, he found his clean boxers. Not normally much for talking while he got dressed, he noted the remarkable quietness inside the bedroom. The bottom right hand corner of the television screen had the word 'MUTE' spelled out in green letters. Grateful for the silence, he finished dressing.

Fully clothed next to her prone, nude body except for his boots, he bent down to give her a kiss. She put a hand against his chest to stop his advance.

"Steve," she said, "We need to talk."

Pulling back, he looked at the clock. He hoped this wouldn't take long. Brenda and the kids would be expecting him soon.

"What's up?"

"Are you satisfied with this?"

"Sure."

"You don't wish sometimes we could have more than this?"

"I don't have time for this shit, Jeannie."

"No, of course you don't. We wouldn't want that precious little wifey of yours to think anything was wrong, now would we?"

Lighting a fresh cigarette, she blew the smoke out in disgust. The tension of her last comment made Steve defensive.

"What the fuck is your problem?"

"I'm sick of this shit. You come here, fuck me, and tell me that I'm ten times the lay your wife is, then I'm alone until you decide to come back."

"You knew what this was. I told you I would never do something as stupid as leave my wife and kids," Steve said. Again he looked toward the clock. He would give her one more minute to make her point, then he was gone.

"I know, I know," she said.

"I've got to go."

"Steve," Jeannie said, "I want more."

"I told you already---"

"Goddamn it! I heard you the first hundred times."

"What the hell is wrong with you?"

"What's wrong with me," Jeannie said, "is that I ain't nothing, but a hole to you."

"Give it a fucking rest already. This is the best I can do."

"I want more, Steve. I'm sick and tired of getting your old lady's leftovers."

"Jeannie, I have to go."

"Good. Get the fuck out of here," she said, "and don't come back unless you can figure it out."

Steve's hands were clenched in rage. Nothing would satisfy him more right now than knocking the shit out of her. Who the fuck was she to make demands on him? Up until this moment, everything had been fine. Women, he thought, if it weren't for pussy men would hunt them like deer.

"I gotta go," he said.

He shoved his boots on without lacing them up and slammed the trailer door behind him. The entire drive home he could hardly concentrate. The thought of not having Jeannie anymore was unacceptable. He was a smart guy. If it killed him, he would figure this shit out.

***

Friday night, Steve and his buddies were exercising their rights as men. Stationed at their usual table, the jukebox couldn't drown out the sound of bowling pins being smashed. The Seven-Ten Split bar set inside of Striker's Bowl-A-Rama had been their hang out since high school. Their great affection with the bar began when the owner had been willing to serve them before they had reached the legal drinking age. As long as they didn't start any trouble and paid in cash, they could get pie-eyed as they liked.

Now as men, the original owner was as distant a memory as those glory days before work and family. They were regular, good customers, who always drank a shitload of draft beer, and settled their tab at last-call.

The four, including Steve, did this as much to decompress as out of habit. Mostly, they told stories about the biggest idiots or some rich asshole they had come across that week. It was a game of one upmanship that lasted from seven until nine. The guy with the best story won by having his tab paid by the others.

Come nine o'clock, the moderately sized bar that could sit thirty snugly was standing room only. The room buzzed as excited people talked, drank shots, and tried to decide what song they would sing. It was a parade of drunken jackasses that got worse as the night wore on. Steve never grew tired of watching people drunkenly slosh off-key through songs, fucking up the lyrics even though they scrolled tele-prompter style on all the big screen TVs.

It was Steve's brother-in-law Vincent who had convinced the current owner to put Karaoke in the bar. Doubling the bar's revenue within two months, he was now putting it on every Friday and Saturday night.

In Steve's opinion, the guy was a loser. The little bit of cash money he made here in two nights was less than he made in one day. He had never known Vincent to have a real job outside of this except little part-time bullshit janitor gigs that paid next to nothing.

Once, mostly due to Brenda's insistence, he had offered Vincent a job as his helper. The son-of-a-bitch turned him down. That was the last time he thought about helping him. If he were on fire, Steve did not believe he would make the effort to piss on him.

Physically, Vincent was repulsive by any sane person's standard. He was a heroin skinny freak. His every bone and joint visible as a skeletons. Deep pock marked ruts in his cheeks from the severe acne he suffered through as a teenager was hideous. He looked more like a survivor of a flash fire than a case of zits. To top it all off, he wore coke-bottle thick glasses due to his insatiable appetite for books. Why the hell a guy would want to read so damn much all the time anyway was a mystery to him? Served the dumb jerk right, Steve thought.

Vincent's hair was long, unkempt, and greasy. The few clothes he owned were pretty much all the same. Stained and ripped blue jeans, a black t-shirt promoting some band no one in the Midwest knew, and the same junky ass Converse high tops that he had worn since Steve had first started dating Brenda.

If Vincent had ever gotten laid, Steve surely thought it was only out of pity. If it weren't for his wife, he wouldn't even say hello to the ugly piece of shit at family get-togethers. Wherever he was, Steve made it a point to keep Vincent in his peripheral vision. If that freak so much as came within twenty feet, he would do his damnedest not to get trapped by him.

Inevitably, he would have no choice but to talk to him.

"Hey, Vince, how's the world treating ya?" Steve would ask.

"You know."

No, I don't know you ignorant asshole that's why I asked.

"How's work?"

"Okay. It's work."

If that's work than I'm a flying fucking elephant.

"Did you see that drunk bitch last Friday? I bet she could have swallowed that mic whole and never gagged."

"Mmm, yeah. I guess. Whatever."

I can't listen to this shit sober.

"I'm gonna get another beer. You want something?"

"Do they have any Diet Pepsi?"

"Not sure, but I'll go look."

Go fuck yourself retard.

That was life with Vincent. Nobody knew what the hell to do with him, but no one had the balls to tell him to fuck off. God knows he wanted to once or twice, but Brenda restrained him. Out of respect for her he left Vincent alone.

As the night wore on, a thought began to formulate inside Steve's drunken mind. Vague at first, the idea became a bit more clear with every beer. If there was ever a way to kill two birds with one stone, this had to be it.

Steve ping-ponged his way down the narrow corridor. He felt acutely proud of himself and was laughing out loud while he pissed. The enormous joy the thought brought couldn't be contained. From a distance, no one would have thought any thing of such behavior. He was merely another guy getting shit faced. It was Steve alone who knew the evil that thrilled him to no end. He left the bar without saying a word to his buddies.

***

The night had turned cold as the waning days of summer gave way to the coming fall weather. Steve's shivered inside his wife's idling mini-van, his light jacket inefficient against the brisk air. To take his mind off the cold, he thought about the plan.

He revved the engine in anticipation as he watched the temperature gauge needle rise from below the capital C. The heat would be refreshing against the sobering cold. Steve turned the blower on halfway. The immediate shock of icy air followed by the mild warmth stopped his chattering teeth. Warm again, he reached into pocket and pulled out his cell phone.

He knew the number he dialed better than his own home phone. It rang five times before Jeannie picked up.

"Hello," she said.

"Hey, baby," Steve said, "did I wake you up?"

"Jesus Christ, Steve. What do you think?"

"Aw, sugar, don't be mad at me."

"I'm not in the mood for this shit, Steve. Some of us have to get up and go to work tomorrow morning. If I'm late one more time it will be my third write up by the nurse this quarter."

"We're kindred souls. I clean shit out of pipes and you wipe it off old folk's asses."

"Kindred souls?"

Steve could hear the familiar sound of her lighter striking flint. He was happy to know she was smoking. It meant she would tolerate his call despite the late hour.

"You have got to be drunk talking that kind of smack."

"I work hard for a living. Nothing wrong with knocking back a few."

"Yeah, right," she said. Jeannie paused to drag on her cigarette. "Did you want to come over?"

"Not tonight, baby."

"So you called me at goddamn near two in the morning to tell me how much you missed me? I'm touched."

"I figured it out."

"Steve, it's late."

"I said," Steve said deliberately louder, "I figured it out."

"Figured out what?" Jeannie asked. Maybe he wasn't as drunk as she initially presumed.

"You said you wanted more. Well, I figured it out."

"Don't fuck with me, Steve."

"Darlin', I wouldn't dream of it."

***

Jeannie slid the magnetic strip through the time-card slot. The laminated plastic rectangle resembled a credit card and doubled as key between the electronically sealed wards. Spared by one minute, she had not been late.

Promptly, Jeannie reported to the nurses' station. Nurse Dugan waited clacking her inch long nails in succession from pinky to pointer. Everyone at the Little Flower Nursing Home knew better than to piss her off. Nurse Dugan had no problem in making a subordinate feel like shit because they had forgotten some minor detail. It was well within her power to reprimand the lower class C.N.A. staff, and it was her delight to do so. The worse of it all was that she held the power of virtual life and death in her slim, ballpoint pen. Jeannie had received only one raise in three years as a direct result of the nurse's evaluations.

Jeannie stood at the nurse's desk. She had learned to wait. Nurse Dugan believed religiously in the proverb that aides should speak only when spoken to. Jeannie tried not to fidget, eager to get in motion, into the rhythm of work.

"Cutting it mighty close there today, Ms. Sitzes."

"Yes, ma'm," Jeannie answered. She made sure to keep direct eye contact. To look away as she spoke was one of Nurse Dugan's many pet peeves.

"Was it car trouble this morning or did we forget to set our alarm?"

"No ma'm."

"Probably spent the entire night carousing with some hoodlum. Someday you'll wind up in some ditch with your throat cut and your legs spread."

"Yes, ma'm."

"Don't sass me. You're lucky to have this job, and I suggest that if you want to keep it you mind your Ps and Qs. Understand?"

"Yes, ma'm."

Nurse Dugan handed a single sheet over the counter to Jeannie that listed room numbers and duties to be performed.

Jeannie took hold of it, but the nurse refused to let it go.

"I'm watching you Ms. Sitzes. Never forget that."

"Yes, ma'm."

Jeannie looked over the sheet as she walked away from the desk. First on the list was an Alzheimer's patient famous for his incontinence. Next was another and then another after that. Nurse Dugan, for reasons unknown to Jeannie, had saw fit to put her on the 'shit run' today. Usually, this sort of thing would have put her into a mood fit to kill. People covered in their own excrement would need to be stripped, bathed, their bed linens changed, and eventually re-dressed. She would dream of the many horrible way she hoped Nurse Dugan would eventually die as her green hospital scrubs became speckled in black and brown dots.

Today, however, she found no discomfort in even these most foul duties. The wonderful idea that Steve proposed had put her into a euphoric trance. She moved room to room with a newfound solace that was the plan.

***

She went after work to buy a new outfit, then spent hours on her hair and make-up while chain smoking. Jeannie hadn't been this nervous in years. If this went well tonight all her hopes of domesticity with Steve may yet come true.

She arrived early at the Seven-Ten Split. Steve had told her to get there around quarter to nine, but she couldn't wait. Even though there was another hour before Karaoke began, the bar was beginning to fill with excited people grabbing the thick, spiral bound books that were all over the place. Jeannie found a seat at the bar and thumbed through one. It was an alphabetical listing of songs. New songs, oldies, pop, punk, metal, country, R&B, and shit she had never heard of before.

"What'll ya have, sweetheart?" the bartender asked.

"Shot of Jager and a Stag if ya got it, a Bud if ya' don't."

Amused by her order, he smiled to himself. He set a twelve-ounce can in front of her next to a shot glass of the black licorice liquor.

In one quick gulp the shot was gone, followed closely by the carbonated tickle of beer. Jeannie was nervous as a whore in church. She immediately ordered another Jager and repeated.

The bartender with the protruding belly and man tits remained. He was still smiling and it was beginning to annoy Jeannie. She was used to strange men's attention, but if this fat asshole thought he had a shot in hell, he was crazy.

"Something funny?" she asked.

"Not necessarily funny ha-ha as just odd."

"Come again?"

"There's only other person to my knowledge who ever orders a Stag with a Jager back around here."

"Who's that?"

"Vincent," the bartender said pointing across the room. "He's the guy in charge of the Karaoke."

Jeannie followed his finger to its target. Vincent had his back turned to toward them.

"Well hell, why didn't you say so? Give me a pair, pal."

Jeannie weaved in-between the tables and people standing about. She almost spilled the drinks more than once, but finally got close enough to tap Vincent's shoulder. The big black hoodie that covered him was puffy. Jeannie had to push much further than she had anticipated before coming into actual contact with his body.

Spooked by the unexpected poke, Vincent turned around. He held a stack of CDs without cases by both hands. For a brief second, Jeannie's mind flashed to a portrait she loved in a coffee-table book titled, "Masterpieces of the Renaissance Age." In this light, with his hood standing at a crisp peak, he looked similar to the picture of a priest contemplating a skull.

Before she could offer him the drinks, he said, "You have to write the song down, then put it in the basket."

"The song?"

Vincent set the silver discs down and showed her a glued three by three-inch notepad. They were request slips on which a person would write down the artist, the song, and their name to be called when it was their turn.

"Here," she said. "You looked thirsty."

Dismayed, he stood still. He had made it a point to remain as invisible as he possibly could. Even though his line of work was dependent on the public, interaction with them was not.

"Okay," he said, "Thanks, I guess."

Vincent set the drinks on a small, separate table void any electronics. He felt awkward as she remained before him. By any man's standards she was beautiful.

"Do you want to sing?"

"Me?" she asked herself. "Aw, hell no. There ain't enough liquor in this bar to do that crazy shit."

"You and me both. I don't know what the hell it is about this stuff that gets these people so excited, but I'm glad it does."

"That's funny," she said, "every time I've been to one of these things the host warms up the crowd."

"I don't do that."

"So why did you buy all this shit," she said panning her drink over the enormous speakers, the black boxes with blinking green and red lights, and a set of four microphones.

"I used to be in a band."

"That's cool," Jeannie said. "What band?"

"Trust me, you never heard of us."

"You doing this until you can get in another band?"

"No," he said. "No more bands. I'm too old for that shit anymore."

"You're never too old to rock-n-roll," Jeannie said. When Vincent didn't respond, she nervously occupied herself by drinking her beer. Undaunted by his lack of enthusiasm towards her she asked, "So this is it now? You just sit back sipping free drinks from Karaoke groupies?" It was meant to be a joke, but Vincent didn't laugh.

"Mostly. Except for the groupies part."

She knew it wasn't meant as a joke. Notwithstanding, she found his self-deprecation amusing.

Her honest laughter was a refreshing change. Vincent's normal defenses fell and before he realized it, he admitted to her something that he had told no one else.

"I write now," he said. A flush of embarrassment struck him. He had suddenly began to sweat underneath the hoodie he used to disguise his unsightly figure and face. "It's weird stuff. Probably nothing anybody will ever read. I've submitted a few short stories to magazines on-line, but whatever. Who gives a shit about art anyway?" Vincent reached for his beer and greedily consumed its cool contents. He knew he needed to shut-up.

The basket that had been littered with a few lone scraps now overflowed with hand written, barely legible requests.

The clock above the bar, set fifteen minutes fast regardless of what bar in America you stood in, signaled Karaoke was about to begin.

"I think I better get started before there's a riot."

"I'm Jeannie," she said with her hand extended, expecting him to be polite and take it.

"What?" he said. It wasn't that he hadn't heard what she said. It was that she had bothered to go this far.

"My- name- is- Jean-nie," she said slowly, as if speaking with a dummy. "What- is- yours?"

This time he laughed.

Her hand was a smaller, but as exceedingly bony as his own. Her palm was smooth yet he could distinguish the raise of calluses against his fingertips. He hoped he was doing this right. It wasn't often beautiful, strange women offered any part of their body to him.

"Me llamo Vincent," he said.

"Como estas, Senior Vincent."

They both laughed.

"Besides good morning, good night, and where's the bathroom, that's all I know," she said.

"Me, too."

"Have a good show."

"Thanks."

Vincent had to force himself to concentrate on his work. Randomly reaching into the basket, he called the first name over the PA and played the music for the requested Conway Twitty tune. While a young, black kid sang pitch perfect to the recording, Vincent scanned the room but could no longer see her.

***

Jeannie sat on a toilet in the ladies room. Her panties around her ankles, two squares of tissues held limply in her hand, she still hadn't peed. The bass thump from the speakers could be heard through the wall, but it was impossible to discern the song that played. Out of habit, she wiped herself, flushing the clean water away.

She stood at a distance from the mirror. Her appearance was fine, perfect as when she had left home. Still, she teased her hair a bit before she washed her hands. Her cell phone twittered to life in her pocket while she dried. She knew who it was before she reached into her skintight denims to answer it.

"Hey, baby," Steve said, "How's it going?"

The background noise of music and other women using the bathroom forced her to put a finger in her open ear to hear him. The normally blunt Steve sounded happy. Not like when he was drunk but more equivalent to having heard a good joke and still amused by it.

Without thinking she answered honestly. "Things are going good. I met Vincent and we talked. He seems nice enough."

Steve's humorous tone vanished. "What the hell are you talking about?"

"What the hell are you talking about?" she rhetorically accused him. "I did exactly what you said to do. I met the guy, introduced myself, and made damn sure I got his attention."

Jesus Christ, Steve thought. He could remember mostly what he had told her last night, despite his disabled state of mind. This, however, was not the reaction expected. He was anticipating a litany of verbal abuse. Something more along the lines of 'How could you do this to me?' or 'Why didn't you tell me this guy was uglier than a gorilla's asshole?'

"What did he think about you?" Steve asked.

"I don't know. He's a weird guy."

"No shit."

"I don't mean weird like creepy, more like it's strange for a smart guy like him to be doing some stupid shit like this for a living. He'd make a better librarian."

Steve couldn't speak. His mind was in overdrive with what she had told him. He had never heard anyone expect for his wife say anything similar about Vincent. He had hoped she would be repulsed, that she would dump this whole idea, and go on happy about the good thing they had leaving behind all this 'wanting more' crap.

"Hello? Hello?" Jeannine asked. Afraid the call might have dropped, she checked the phone's display. Five incremental bars clearly showed the connection held strong. Jeannie placed the phone back to her ear. "Are you still there? I can't hear you nod, Steve."

"Yeah," he said, "Sorry about that. I was thinking."

"I can barely hear you," Jeannie lied. Nothing pissed her off more than when Steve became distant.

"I'll see ya tomorrow then."

"What?" she yelled, pretending she couldn't hear him.

"I said I'll see---"

Jeannie closed the phone and turned off the power. What the fuck his problem was, it was his alone. This was all his idea. If she could get Vincent's virgin ass interested, she would be in like Flint. Birthday parties, Fourth of July's, Thanksgivings, and Christmases could be theirs to share. So what if it was all a game. She had no problem with fucking one guy while using another.

She laughed as she walked back into the dimly lit barroom. An obese, young woman was grinding out Alanis Morrisette's 'You Oughta Know' complete with lyrical pantomime. She was drunk, and there was no doubt that somebody had recently broken her heart. If one of these derelicts played his cards right tonight, there was no doubt she would let him fuck her fat brains out.

Jeannie saw Vincent behind her. He sat as sullen as Poe's raven upon his bust, ready for her to finish. A white slip in his hand, prepared to call out the next in line, he saw Jeannie at the bar. With a shrug, he smiled at her. She smiled back, pretending to gag herself with her finger in reference to the singer. Once again, they both laughed.

***

The Waffle House at two-thirty in the morning was a funhouse without mirrors. After the Seven-Ten Split closed, Jeannie had waited for Vincent. It didn't take much to put away the mics and tarp the PA speakers. The restaurant was busy, but they were quickly seated. A hostess, adorned in a brown head kerchief, presumed them a couple and escorted them to a booth. The table was hardly able to accommodate one meal, much less two. Without a moment's hesitation, they ordered coffee and pancakes.

In the meantime, though still surrounded by drunks, the noise became senseless. Occasionally spikes of other people's conversations made it impossible to hear the jukebox.

The light inside was a drastic change from the bar. It was bright, dispelling all shadows. Vincent was sure whatever illusion had been upheld in the bar's dimness by this woman would certainly be eradicated by the restaurant's unforgiving illumination. Jeannie ironically felt the same way of herself.

Where Vincent was self-conscious of his unkempt hair and red scarred cheeks, Jeannie wished she could reapply her make-up. With no recourse for their individual appearances, they drank their coffee slowly to avoid talking.

The waitress brought their order, then hurried to the next. It was the bar rush and most of the customers were fairly intoxicated. The best thing to keep the retches satisfied was hot food and lots of coffee served with lightning efficiency. There was nothing worse than a hungry, drunken asshole.

Jeannie chose the strawberry-flavored syrup. It had been hours since she had last eaten and each bite seemed to make her hungrier for the next.

Vincent smiled as the red sap dribbled down the sides of her chin.

Jeannie looked up at him. Through a mouthful of pancakes, she asked, "What?"

"Nothing," he said.

***

The car would not start. Vincent had connected the jumper cables, revved his engine, but an hour and a quarter tank of gas later it was simple. The battery was dead.

Jeannie sat in the van's passenger seat. Except for the two front seats there was nothing inside. The floor in the rear was covered by a piece of misshapen carpet that was obviously recycled from the dumpsters. With its tinted black windows and all steel sides, it was the kind of vehicle she had spent her whole life avoiding.

She had cracked her window and was smoking after having asked Vincent's permission. He said he could care. Jeannie could clearly hear the car's uncooperative click, click, click. She knew it was a lost cause before he told her.

Back inside the van, Vincent held his hands over the vents like a campfire. His pale skin had reddened from the cold.

"I guess I should call a cab," Jeannie said.

"That's stupid," Vincent said. It instantaneously struck him how asinine his comment sounded. "I'm sorry, I didn't mean you were stupid. I meant---"

"I know what you meant, but I don't exactly live around here."

"That's cool. I don't mind, but on the other hand…"

Jeannie closely eyed him. She didn't need a picture drawn for her to know what he was thinking.

"How far is your place?"

"Maybe ten minutes down the road. It's not the Taj Mahal, but it's decent."

"What the hell," Jeannie said, "let's go."

***

Vincent's apartment was a typical one-bedroom bachelor's place. Jeannie stood in the middle of the front room from which if she took two steps to her right she would be the kitchen. A small square area a blind man wouldn't call a hallway was divided by two doors. Both doors wide open revealed an extremely sparse bedroom and a fairly clean bathroom.

The walls of the apartment were decorated thoroughly in posters for metal bands, gore movies, and occasionally a photo of Vincent. The latter being was what she found interesting. While he busied himself, trying to pick up empty beer cans and dirty clothes, she compared the guy he was then with who he was now. In the pictures he wore white face paint with red streaks meant to look like dripping blood. His strawberry blonde hair had been dyed coal black. In every picture he looked so serious, but so did the three other guys she presumed to be the remainder of the band. Despite the make-up and the sourpuss expressions, she could tell they were young kids then, having the time of their lives. Jeannie wished she had something like this as a watermark to her life. Since leaving home at seventeen, she had done nothing to speak of unless you counted having two abortions as something to be proud.

Vincent came into the front room with a pillow, a sheet, and a blanket. She was mildly ashamed of the assumption she had made in the van. It was refreshing that there were still some men in this world who didn't expect what she had grown accustomed to giving in trade. She had never felt safer alone with a man.

Finished with the couch, Jeannie was blown away by his skill. She thought even Nurse Dugan would approve of the tidy bed he had assembled.

Vincent, though, seemed edgy. Something was on his mind, something important enough that Jeannie figured he'd let the cat out of the bag soon enough. Relaxed, she sat on her freshly made bed, waiting on him to either speak his piece or bid her goodnight.

Out of habit, she set a cigarette to her lips, then paused with her lighter before her face. "Mind if I smoke?"

"Now, that's funny," Vincent said. He opened pair of doors below his meager television, pulled out a tray, and set it on the coffee table. A pipe obviously used to smoke marijuana and a sandwich baggie full of the stuff lay before them both. "I was going to ask you the same thing."

"Vincent," she said, "I never thought I would be so happy my car broke down in my whole life."

After four bowls apiece, Jeannie couldn't remember going to sleep.

***

The next afternoon she awoke with the start of awaking a foreign place. She stepped to the bathroom, took an enormous pee, swabbed her mouth out with toothpaste using her finger to brush, and came back to the couch.

She could see Vincent from where she sat sleeping face down on his bed. He was still fully clothed except for his bare feet. It was more a surprise to her she hadn't woke up next him than on his comfortable couch.

Jeannie grabbed for her cigarettes that were lying next to the dope tray. She enjoyed as much as needed that first daily hit of nicotine as she deeply inhaled. The sun was full and bright, but did not enter against the turned blinds. Jeannie could hear the cars regularly pass on the nearby highway and she wondered what time it might be.

She found her pants under the blanket, theorizing she must have removed them while she slept. The phone was still lodged in her right front pocket. Jeannie held the power button for one second and waited for the digital display to appear. The phone's clock read one-eighteen p.m., this however, she did not find disconcerting. What alarmed her was the icon for her voicemail blinking full.

Jeannie punched another button and held the phone to her ear. A feminized robot voice announced, "Message one," followed by a short beep. It was Steve. Pushing the number three, the same robot voice told her, "Message erased. Message two." It was Steve and again, she deleted without listening. By the time she had opened the thirtieth voicemail, she disconnected from her messages by pressing the red button marked 'END.' He had called every ten minutes since she had hung up on him in the ladies room. The few messages she had actually listened to, he was drunk. Served him right she thought. Until there was a ring on her left hand, she was free to do what she pleased. She hoped he was in agony right now, the same kind she experienced every time she sat like a goddamn dog at her window waiting on him to come Sunday mornings.

The phone rang before she had thought to tun the power off. It's ring-tone seemed loud in the still apartment. In an effort not to awaken Vincent, she quickly answered. It was no mystery to her who was calling.

"Hello," she said.

"Where the fuck are you?" Steve demanded.

"None of your business."

"You fucking whore!"

"Fuck you. Remember whose idea this shit was to begin with."

She noticed Vincent had begun to stir. Jeannie had been trying to be quiet, but found it particularly difficult not to be led by her emotions with Steve.

Vincent was definitely awake. Propped up on his elbows, he smiled at the sight of her.

Jeannie pointed to the phone and mouthed 'my mom' to him. He shook his head, something between saying he understood and whatever. Out of his bed, he went to the bathroom. Even with the door closed, she could hear the strong sound of his urination. It took her a second re-focus on her phone conversation.

Steve hadn't stopped talking. She heard him say, "trailer," reclaiming her attention to his futile rant.

"Two hours I waited and called and waited before I fucking knew it. I had no choice, but to go back home. Now I'm fucking stuck at my kids' basketball game."

"So what," she said.

"So what? I'll tell you so what, bitch. This thing ends now. It was a stupid idea anyhow."

"I don't think so," she said. "In fact, I think its probably one of the smartest things you've ever done."

"Fuck me!" Steve yelled in disgust. "You slept with him, didn't you?"

"None of your business."

"Quit fucking saying that."

She could hear in the background somebody chastise him for his language. In typical Steve style, she could hear him respond to the anonymous do-gooder with a vibrant, "Go fuck yourself."

Vincent came out of the bathroom and stood in the hall. Too polite to interrupt, he had the good manners to wait until she was done.

"Mom," Jeannie said, "I have to go."

"Mom?" Steve asked. "What the fuck Je---"

"I love you, too."

Promptly, she closed the phone and turned off the power. Steve was no doubt calling her back this instant. His sudden neediness was both disturbing and emasculating. It gave her a secret pleasure to think that big, bad Steve, the manly plumber man had been reduced to acting like a little bitch.

"How's your mom?" Vincent asked with a hint of facetiousness.

Jeannie laughed and lit up a smoke. "She's going to be okay."

***

Jeannie took a shower and changed into clothes Vincent lent to her. His standard uniform of jeans and a t-shirt fit her fairly well. The pants were a bit tight, but she hoped the over-sized t-shirt hid her muffin top. She had never worn men's clothing in public before, yet she felt oddly empowered.

They smoked a joint in the van as Vincent drove. It didn't take Jeannie long to figure Vincent smoked a lot of weed. That was certainly all right by her. It was an inconsequential drug in her opinion and if given the choice between alcohol and pot, she would choose weed every time.

By the time they had arrived at the auto parts store, they were thoroughly stoned. Jeannie was pretty sure the sales clerk knew. He was cool about it though and while it seemed to be an effort for her to recall the make and model of her car, he seemed pleased to help them. Vincent paid for the battery, insisted on it, and Jeannie found his chivalry quaint.

Starved, they ordered tacos and hamburgers at a Jack-In-The-Box drive thru. The greasy food tempered their collective buzz. Jeannie applied hot sauce to his deep fried Mexican treats while he drove. She told him she didn't mind, that it would be far better if he could fully concentrate on the road considering their current mental conditions. In truth, she wanted to return some of his kindness. He had done so much for her and hadn't made even a furtive pass toward her. It was rare to be so appreciated and she couldn't help herself for liking it.

Her buzz pretty well disposed, she watched as Vincent installed her new battery. He worked methodically, doing one thing at a time, careful as a surgeon with the greasy car.

Vincent started the car without any hesitation. He closed the hood and climbed back into the van's driver seat. Through the windshield they watched the car idle. It was funny to Jeannie. Her car was fixed, but she had no desire to leave.

Vincent asked, "You got a boyfriend?"

"No," she said thinking about Steve. The last two years seemed vulgar in comparison to the few hours she had been with Vincent. Steve was right in calling her a whore. She was his whore.

Jeannie found a scrap piece of paper in her small purse and a pen. She wrote her number down for him and handed it over.

Vincent couldn't keep from smiling. The ten digits might as well been the winning lottery numbers to him. With precision, he inserted the jaggedly ripped paper in his billfold.

"I guess I better get going," she said. "It has been a long night and I had better get some rest before work tomorrow."

"I'll call you."

"You better."

Jeannie leaned over the seat and rested her body weight between the steering wheel and the back of Vincent's seat. With delicate restraint, she kissed his rutted cheek. Through her lips she could feel him trembling.

She worried as she left the van and went to her car. He hadn't looked at her or said a word. Behind her own steering wheel she mustered the courage to look one last time at Vincent. He was staring directly at her.

He put his hand to his lips, kissed the tips of his fingers, and blew a kiss toward her. Jeannie reached up and pretended to grab it. After a lifetime of being with men, of seeing their naked exposed flesh upon her own, this was the closest thing to intimacy she had ever experienced.

***

Monday was busier than usual at work. Two of the other girls had called in sick, and Jeannie was forced to do the work of three people. Not impossible, but exhausting none the less. The only highlight was that it also kept Nurse Dugan too busy to ride her ass.

Jeannie drove home at a break neck speed. Her pathetic stereo system cranked as loud as it would go, she loudly sang along with the radio to relieve the day's stress. She hoped there wasn't any cops between her and home. If she got another speeding ticket, there was a hell of a good chance she would lose her license. Fuck it, she thought.

She was tired, hungry, and desperate to clean the elderly stench from her body.

The surprise she found when she pulled into the driveway dumbfounded her. Red, long-stemmed roses in half a dozen vases covered the steps leading to her front door. Their magnificent, overwhelming aroma dwarfed her body odor. She caressed a handful of buds to prove to herself she was not hallucinating. The petals were softer than an infant's skin and without warning she began to cry.

It took her half an hour to carry them all inside. The interior of her dingy trailer looked like a display at Shaw's Garden.

A green ribbon attached a tiny envelope to one rose. Carefully she loosened it from the flower and read the card inside.

The penmanship was obviously printed by a computer, but the sentiment was from a romantic's heart.

"There are many beautiful things, but the silent beauty of a flower surpasses them all." S. Teshigahara

They were from Vincent. There was no doubt in her regarding that. This sure as hell wasn't something Steve could even fathom doing.

Surrounded by her private garden, Jeannie sat in the middle of the floor. The magnificence was surreal. Was this what they called love? She didn't know, but if it was, Jeannie couldn't imagine a more wonderful thing.

***

Steve was in hell. That ungrateful cunt, Jeannie, how could she do this to him?

He had been lucky enough to bid a job in Chesterfield that would last him all week. The affluent home set among the rolling hills, abutting to a golf course that had hosted several PGA tournaments, would pay handsomely for work that was simple enough. The home had six bathrooms and the owners wanted each re-fitted with custom vanity hardware. Of course, it also meant the removal and installation of six commodes as well. The most challenging aspect would be in the lady of the home's personal powder room. In addition to a regular toilet, she had insisted on a matching bidet. That was what would take the majority of his time. The sum total he would collect from this job was almost embarrassing by his standards.

This kind of a job would normally put him a terrific mood, but he couldn't help himself. Every minute of his day was consumed with her. He was having constant flashbacks to their sex, her body pleasing his every wanton pleasure.

After Sunday, he had been drinking heavily every night. His usual four or five beers a night became twelve accompanied by half a bottle of tequila or whiskey. The bitch of it all was he drank to forget, yet it only intensified the remorse.

He woke up Brenda Monday night desperate for sex. Not with her, but with Jeannie. In the darkness he kept his eyes closed, drunkenly imagining his mistress' body under him. Tuesday, he did the same but did not enjoy it. Brenda complained mostly through the motions, and his ability to fantasize his lover presence couldn't be accomplished. Disappointed with Brenda's cooperation, he masturbated in the basement, using his wife's dirty panties for inspiration.

Each morning though he awoke more depressed than the last. Work a chore to be faced with no hope to escape his constant misery. He thought if he could just talk with her, not on the phone, but face-to-face. Maybe he could reason with her. He wasn't above using every cent made on this job to bribe her back if he had to. The only thing he wouldn't put on the table in trade was himself.

He had a twenty-year strong marriage. Without Brenda and his children, he would probably kill himself. A sin even he didn't believe God would absolve him from. That kind of thinking though wasn't like him. Up until all this shit hit the fan, he was happy guy. No, the rational thought, the idea that replaced the longing for Jeannie, was that of her death.

Throughout the day he imagined shooting her, strangling her, watching her sit inside of that shitty little car of hers as it exploded, or throwing her off the Eads Bridge. At night he drank and mourned for her, whipping himself with alcohol for his errant thoughts and cursing himself for doing such a stupid thing.

By Friday, with a check in his wallet, he drove with determination to the Seven-Ten Split. It was four o'clock and happy hour didn't begin until six. Fuck it, Steve thought. He couldn't take another night at home with Brenda or without Jeannie.

***

Vincent made it to the bar at eight sharp. This last week with Jeannie was the best he had ever known. Everyday he talked with Jeannie after she got home from work. He listened patiently as she vented about her job, her home, and her life in general.

She returned the favor as Vincent regaled her with stories from the being in a band. Mostly, they were funny, entertaining tid-bits she couldn't imagine having really happened, but he told them so matter-of-factly, Jeannie had no reason to doubt their validity.

One of his most charming was the time the band was flat broke in Iowa. Out of desperation for gas money, they worked out a deal to clean the bar they had just gigged at for gas money. After two days of stealing beer and beef jerky, the owner called the police. The small town Sheriff impounded their van and locked them together in a cell with two bunks and a stainless steel commode.

Unable to pay their meager fines, the Sheriff gave them a choice: Play a charity gig at the local high school or pick trash off the side of the highway for a month. "It was always some shit like that," Vincent told Jeannie, melancholy for those carefree days, but not the desperation it bred.

Steve's buddies were at their regular table sans his brother-in-law. That didn't concern him. Vincent had seen Brenda's mini-van in the parking lot. Steve was here somewhere, probably in the john or pumping dollars into the impossible to beat claw machine. His brother-in-law's presence use to concern him. They had never bonded and it was obvious Steve wanted nothing to do with him. Vincent, in turn, was more than willing to accommodate his wishes.

It took Vincent less than fifteen minutes to set the songbooks out and power up the equipment. It was his ritual to check every microphone prior to the show. Whether it was necessary or not, he replaced each wireless' nine volt battery source. There had been thus far only one time a mic went dead during a performance. The singer had been malleable regarding the whole incident and was glad to take it again from the top. Vincent, however, found it professionally embarrassing. If he could, it was a mistake he would do his damnedest not to repeat.

Out of the corner of his eye, he saw Steve stumble into his buddies' table as he was sound checking the first mic.

"Check one. Check one-two," he announced.

"Check this mother fucker!" Steve said to the great amusement of his pals. He held his crotch with his right and shook it with enthusiasm toward Vincent.

Vincent picked up the next mic. It's green light glowed in the darkness indicating full power.

"Check one. Check one-two," Vincent repeated. Before he could put it down, Steve was beside him. A thick odor of alcohol radiated from his every pore. Hardly able to stand, Steve rested his body into Vincent.

"I want to sing," Steve said. His speech was a mixture of slur and beer belches.

"Sure, Steve," Vincent said trying to seem undaunted. "Just give me a second."

Behind Steve and his buddies, Vincent could see the bartender. He watched from behind the bar with the look of a dog ready to attack.

"No goddamn it. I want to sing now," Steve said. With a slight bit of resistance from Vincent, Steve pulled the mic from his grip.

"Okay," Vincent said elongating upon the vowel, "what song do you want?"

Into the microphone, Steven yelled, "What it's gonna be fellas?"

"Brittany Spears," yelled one of men. Another, even louder called, "Madonna."

The reckless goading by Steve's friends made Vincent nervous. It was obvious they had all been drinking more than usual. In an attempt to sandbag their current taunts, which could easily turn from playfulness to cruelty, Vincent cued up Black Sabbath's 'Ironman.' A shout of ecstasy erupted from the table as Steve shouted, "Fuck yeah!" into the microphone.

Gray words scrolled turning white as the lyrics appeared on the TV's. Unable to read the legible words through his inebriated haze, Steve lyrically imitated the words in an infantile fashion of unintelligible grunts.

"Bluh, bluh, ba-boo-bee. Dada dada, dada, Fuck this shit."

Vincent tried to control the volume from the mixer, but the squeal of feedback accentuated Steve's ever-increasing volume. Frustrated, worried that Steve's close proximity to the massive speaker could cause a blowout, he futilely moved the mixer's sliders lower trying to avoid disaster.

It was a shock to everyone when the bartender pushed Steve from behind. Too drunk to stand, he fell with no more effort of a wobbly domino to the floor. The microphone slammed to the concrete floor causing a loud pop that overloaded the speakers. The built-in clip mechanism automatically shut down the power in an effort to save itself.

Steve floundered on the floor trying to regain his footing. He had not realized he had been pushed until he rolled over from his stomach to his back. Even in his worthless state, it was apparent to him things had become deadly serious.

The voices of his buddies became quiet with reverence. The unmistakable sound of a twelve-gauge shotgun click-chuck slide action was robust in the soundless room. Vincent was grateful for the intervention, but immobile with fear at the sight.

"That's enough," the bartender said. He was aiming the shotgun at a forty-five degree angle to the ceiling. Without hesitation, he could put the barrel onto a target. At this range, whatever he aimed at he could hit with complete confidence.

"Fuck almighty, man. There ain't no need for that kinda shit. We were just having fun. Ain't that right, Vince?" Steve asked.

Vincent couldn't have said shit if he had a mouthful. He had seen Steve plenty drunk on many occasions. Normally a solitary drunk, who preferred the company of an empty, dark corner, it was rare to see him driven so far over the edge. Strangely enough, he did want to help him, to pick him up, and defend his actions as the carelessness we all befell to in the name of relaxation. The serious bartender and his weapon rendered him mute.

"Well, ain't this some kind of fuck you," Steve said.

"There's a cab outside. I suggest you give up your keys and get your ass home."

Steve floundered to his feet and found his balance against a chair. His friends whispered among themselves, unable to hide their laughing smirks. Steve smiled at them, emboldened, not understanding that for a change he was the butt of the joke.

"You can kiss my ass you dumb, fat bastard."

Enraged, the bartender swung the barrel of the shotgun with the precision of hitting a fastball. Steve collapsed unconscious as he crumpled to the floor.

Before his buddies could rush him, the bartender swung the weapon directly toward them. Steve had got what was coming to him. If any of them decided to play hero, it might be the last thing they ever did.

The trio stood stopped in motion, paused in their group reaction to retaliate.

The biggest guy spoke for the group with his hands held high above his head. "We don't want any trouble."

"Then pick this piece of shit up and get the hell out of my bar."

The group moved slowly toward Steve. Limp and unconscious, they carried his slumped body outside.

"You okay, kid?" The bartender asked Vincent.

"Yeah," he said having to think about it.

The bartender rested his gun over his shoulder and let go a deep sigh of relief.

"These fucking guys. Always horsing around, they never know when to quit."

Vincent bent down and collected the fragments of the mic. The bulbous silver knob had a large dent and a wide crack split halfway down the cylindrical case. He didn't need to test it to know it was a total loss.

The bartender set his hand on Vincent's shoulder. He too could tell the damage to the microphone was beyond repair.

"Maybe," the bartender said, "we should call it a night. The cops will be here soon enough."

***

Sunday was a beautiful day. The forecast for cloudy weather had been circumvented by an unprecedented warm front out of the south. Late October's traditional cold being held at bay was almost a disappointment to the heavily bundled guests.

It was an established ritual for the Bickel family, Vincent's family, to hold a party the weekend prior to Halloween. Mother and Father Bickel, the proud parents of five, and beaming grandparents of nine found comfort in the ritual of gathering. The children played upstairs, enjoying video games on Grandpa's colossal TV and a buffet of homemade candies and cookies dutifully prepared by Grandma. The adults were given the secluded semi-privacy of the basement.

The vibrant yellow gold shag carpeting had faded. It's luster fresh and new in the seventies was now dull, stained, and quite immaterial to the décor. Concrete basement walls were disguised behind imitation pressed wood paneling. Cutouts where once a light switch had been installed then removed or access had to be gained to make a repair were left open. Not forgotten necessarily, but familiar enough that after a time they were no longer noticeable.

Its only modernization in the last twenty-five years was a state of the art stereo system. Eight speakers had been snugly retrofitted to the ceiling, inconspicuous to the eye and warm to the ear. Dad insisted Vincent not play any of that modern rap-crap and he had gladly complied. For this party in particular, he had chosen a mix of classic soul featuring the likes of Al Green and Bill Withers. It proved a pleasant change of pace from his normal Rolling Stones and Grateful Dead picks.

Jeannie and Vincent sat together at the makeshift bar, occupying two of the three available stools. The remainder of the group compiled of blood relatives to distant cousins, mingled or danced or sat on a graveyard of old couches. All were accounted for except for Brenda and Steve.

"I enjoyed the movie the other night," Jeannie said.

"Me, too."

Vincent and Jeannie had missed the last third of the movie to sit in the back row and make-out like lustful teenagers.

They had mutually decided to take it slow. Sex, if it should come to pass, wouldn't be a perfunctory, routine thing. Vincent had had a lifetime worth of anonymous sex with pathetic groupies eager to get closer to a band. Likewise, Jeannie in a desperate attempt to erase her multiple and abusive stepfathers, was in no rush to consummate this wonderful thing. When the time was right, they would know it and together they would gently cross that border.

The shock on Jeannie's face was apparent as everyone else's when Brenda and Steve came downstairs. Steve with stitches and a swollen black eye was already somewhat drunk. Without the slightest hesitation, he left his wife alone to find more liquor. Brenda, used to such behavior dismissed his actions as routine.

Her coat still on, she walked directly toward Vincent and embraced him in a full hug. Jeannie found the resemblance striking. Except for her smooth cheeks and her full-figured body, she and Vincent were identical twins. After exchanging pleasantries, Vincent modestly introduced Jeannie to his sister.

Without any hesitation, Brenda embraced her. A bolt of shame and regret twisted at Jeannie's heart knowing what she had done with this woman's husband. Not understanding her embarrassment, Vincent misinterpreted her sudden reclusive spirit as a simple case of nerves. Who wouldn't be uncomfortable at first, he rationalized, meeting someone's entire family for the first time.

Vincent offered to take Brenda's coat. He surreptiously hoped that it would give the women an opportunity to get to know each other.

"How long have you been seeing, Vincent?"

"A couple of weeks now," Jeannie replied. Her concentration wasn't effected as much by the few drinks she had consumed as much by her awareness Steve was watching them.

"You make a cute couple. When Vincent first told me about you, I was so happy for him. It's been a long time since he's had someone special."

"Well," she said feeling genuinely demure, "I think Vincent is pretty special too."

Vincent came back and placed his arm about Jeannie's midsection. She found it comforting that he could be so casual with her in this atmosphere. Her only regret was to the clandestine set of circumstances that had allowed her such a marvelous fortune.

Jeannie excused herself from Vincent's embrace to use the bathroom. It was across the room, at the far end, a direction impossible to cross over without passing by Steve.

She maneuvered between family members. Hard to be heard over the music, she politely tapped strangers on the shoulder to pass by. The bathroom door closed a moment before she came to it and she would have to wait her turn. Jeannie's urge wasn't critical and she easily could wait the few minutes before it would become her turn.

"Hey, baby," Steve said. He was close to her and his presence surprised Jeannie.

"Oh, hey, Steve," she said. "Great party, huh?"

"Cut the shit, bitch."

"Steve, I don't think---"

"Fuck what you think. How much longer are you going to keep doing this?"

"Doing what?" She smiled pretending Steve said something amusing. Jeannie looked over his shoulder toward Vincent, hoping to catch his attention.

"You listen to me," Steve said, "I'm sorry, okay? I'm sorry, and I'll do anything you want."

"I don't want anything from you."

"I'm serious goddamn it. Let's go somewhere for the weekend. We can get a nice room at some bed and breakfast, order room service, do whatever you like. Quit ignoring me, baby. I can't take another night without you."

Jeannie smiled and waved to Vincent over Steve's shoulder. Through her smile, she said, "It's over."

"It is, is it?"

"That's right asshole and you don't have anyone to blame except your own dumb self."

"Maybe I should tell pizza face about what a slut you are?"

"Go ahead," Jeannie said. The bathroom door opened and she stepped inside. "I don't give a fuck whether you do or you don't. I'm not the one who is going to lose shit. Think about it, Steve."

She closed the door in his face and locked the handle.

Steve backed away from the door in shock. His every threat had been futile. Of course he wouldn't say anything. She knew that and now he knew it too.

Next week was Halloween, the month after that Thanksgiving, and then Christmas, New Year's Eve, and so on. Steve cursed himself at what a perfect idiot he had been.

Jeannie was right that it was over. He could accept that it was the truth simply because there wasn't any other reasonable alternatives. Besides, he consoled himself, it was only a matter of time before another trailer park whore came along.

About the Author

Joe Schwartz is a lifetime resident of St. Louis. He has lived as far south of the city as Hillsboro and as far north as St. Charles.

He has been variously employed as an offshore oil rig worker, a paralegal, a home delivery driver, and is currently employed with the St. Louis Public Library.

Joe lives in High Ridge, Missouri with his wife of fifteen years and their two children.